THE UNEXPECTED GIFT

When London nurse Megan Falstaff is informed she's received an inheritance from her beloved godmother Cathleen, she's expecting a couple of cat figurines. What she actually inherits is a boarding cattery in the village of Little River — with the stipulation that she must run it for at least a year. Getting to grips with the eccentricities of felines and village folk alike is challenging for Megan — and matters aren't helped by the disdain of the haughty vet Doctor William Wakefield . . .

Books by Sarah Purdue
in the Linford Romance Library:

STANDING THE TEST OF TIME
PLANNING FOR LOVE
LOVE'S LANGUAGE
TRUSTING A STRANGER
LOVE UNEXPECTED
PLAYING MUM

SARAH PURDUE

THE UNEXPECTED GIFT

Complete and Unabridged

LINFORD
Leicester

First published in Great Britain in 2017

First Linford Edition
published 2018

A catalogue record for this book is available
from the British Library.

ISBN 978–1–4448–3781–0

Published by
F. A. Thorpe (Publishing)
Anstey, Leicestershire

Set by Words & Graphics Ltd.
Anstey, Leicestershire
Printed and bound in Great Britain by
T. J. International Ltd., Padstow, Cornwall

This book is printed on acid-free paper

1

'Er, Mr. McKinley, I think there may have been a mix-up.'

'Really?' Mr. McKinley fixed his pince-nez glasses as low down his nose as was possible without them falling off. 'You are Miss Megan Falstaff, are you not?'

Megan flushed, feeling suddenly as if she were consulting a solicitor because she had committed a terrible crime.

'Yes, but I was expecting to come for the reading of Cathleen Somers' will.'

Mr. McKinley raised a white eyebrow. 'Yes, that's correct.'

Megan looked around in confusion, as if expecting to see Auntie Cath's family somehow appear from behind the book-laden shelves or the tall plant holder. 'But . . . where is everyone else?'

Now Mr. McKinley looked slightly bemused. 'Everyone else?'

'Yes, the rest of Auntie Cath's — I mean, Cathleen's — family.'

Mr. McKinley put his hands together and laid them on the blotter pad on his desk.

'Ah, I see, then. I imagine Cathleen never told you.'

Megan was too stunned to say anything; she simply shook her head. Mr. McKinley smiled warmly.

'My dear, you are Cathleen's sole beneficiary.'

It was a full thirty seconds before Megan realised that she was holding both her breath and the arms of her chair — the last, so tightly that her knuckles had turned white. Mr. McKinley let her be, but pressed a button on his desk and requested that his assistant bring them some tea.

Megan allowed her breath out. Her brain had completely shut down and resolutely refused to function. So instead she concentrated on breathing.

'How do you like your tea, Miss Falstaff?'

'Milk, one sugar,' she answered woodenly as she automatically took the cup and saucer when it was offered. She forced herself to look at McKinley before she took a sip of hot tea.

'Better?' he asked kindly.

Megan nodded. 'Yes. I'm sorry, it was just a bit of a shock. I thought Auntie Cath would have left me some figurine cats or something.'

'Well, she did, my dear — but she also left you the four-bedroom bungalow and the display case that they are kept in, as well as her thriving business.'

Megan tried to comprehend the news, but she still couldn't accept it. It wasn't right.

'But what about Auntie Cath's family?' She put her fingers to her lips as she realised that she had said this out loud. She remembered all the times as a child that she had asked Auntie Cath about her family, and always been distracted by one of her relative's elaborate stories of her favourite cat's latest adventures. 'I mean, she must have had a family?'

Mr. McKinley smiled, but Megan noticed the sadness pulling at the corners of his eyes.

'Yes, she did, but they were not close. Cathleen always said that you were her favourite person in the whole world, and in reality she didn't like that many people.'

Megan felt the grief awaken in the hole in her chest. 'You knew Auntie Cath?' she asked, determined to distract herself.

'Yes. I've known her since we were children: our fathers were partners in this law firm.' He waved his arms around expansively. 'She was a very unique woman.'

Megan nodded, not trusting herself to speak at that moment.

'Do her family know? About me, I mean? What if they decide to challenge it . . . I mean, they were her relatives . . . surely they have a right to . . . '

Mr. McKinley walked around to the front of his desk and placed a reassuring hand on Megan's arm.

'You leave all of that to me, Miss Falstaff. Please believe me when I tell you that this is what Cathleen wanted. I drew up the will myself. Her family will not bother you, I promise.'

Megan glanced up and saw darkness pass fleetingly across the solicitor's face, to be quickly replaced by the kindly smile. He patted her arm one last time before returning to his seat on the other side of his desk.

'There are some details and some conditions, if you feel up to discussing them now — or, alternatively, we can arrange another date?'

Megan took a deep breath and forced a smile.

'Now is fine, thank you.'

* * *

Megan wound down the window of her new car, taking deep breaths of London-free air. It had been a bit of a dodgy start. She hadn't driven since she had moved to London seven years ago, and when the car salesman had said driving was like riding a bike — you never forget — he clearly had never seen her drive before. So she had been subjected to a monotonous lecture on which pedal was the clutch and which was the brake and how important it was not to mix up the two — as if she couldn't figure that part out herself.

Kangaroo-jumping down Peckham High Street with a bunch of car salesman looking on was not, possibly, the best start to her day, but it was definitely improving. She had driven straight back to her flat — remembering all the while the reason why she had relied on public transport for seven years — to pick up the last few bits of her London life. With a car filled to the roof with cardboard boxes and carrier bags, and relying only on her wing mirrors, she wound her way slowly south of the river. Her furniture and the rest of her life was already in storage, to give her time to figure out her next move.

Megan drove into Little River past the welcome sign complete with 'Population 1,092', wondering as usual if that number included farmyard animals and pets. Little River was situated deep in the East Sussex countryside, and was essentially all that remained of the estate of Lord Markington. The Manor House had been sold many years previously, but not without much grumbling from local residents, as it had been turned into luxury apartments frequented by London stockbrokers and their beautiful girlfriends. This in turn had encouraged a London set of shops and a wine bar to appear out of nowhere in a village that had previously prided itself on having one traditional pub and a post office, circa 1817.

Auntie Cath's bungalow was about two miles outside of the village centre (if you could call it that), and had been built on the site of a farm labourer's cottage. The bungalow had a couple of acres of land, and it was from here she had launched her business venture:

'Cath's Cats', an upmarket cattery specifically aimed at the county set who liked to weekend in London and take long exotic vacations.

Cath's Cats — Megan still could not quite believe that she was now the proud owner of a cattery. She quite liked cats in the way that most non-cat-owners feel about felines. She had never owned a cat, or even had a stray one as a lodger, but had decided in the last few weeks that they could be no worse than the difficult patients and their more troublesome relatives from her time as a nurse. She still couldn't quite believe that she had walked away from her job and her life in London, but she had. She was sure, based on the will, that Auntie Cath had thought it would do her good. And, as always, Auntie Cath was probably right.

2

Megan pulled her car into the long gravel drive and tucked it in behind a shiny white mini-people-carrier with 'Cath's Cats — Cattery to the Stars' painted on one side. It was her minivan now. She fought the urge to pinch herself — the whole situation was too surreal.

Stepping out of her car, she closed the door and took in the bungalow. It was traditionally built and had a well-cared for look about it. The borders were neat and weeded, and the gravel was so orderly in appearance that it made Megan wonder if she was expected to rake it to make it look so.

She felt in her pocket for the spare set of keys that Mr. McKinley had given her, and walked up to the front door. For a moment she half-expected the door to be flung open and for her to be enveloped in a bear hug. As she unlocked the door and pushed it open, she felt as if it were frozen in time. Auntie Cath was really gone, her constant loving presence in her life had disappeared, and Megan felt the sense of loss she had been suppressing well up inside of her. She didn't try to hold back the tears, but let them flow as she wandered around the different rooms, remembering. She had always felt truly at home here, but now she felt like an uninvited guest. Everything was exactly like it had been when she had last visited, but seemed somehow alien now it all belonged to her. It felt like she was trespassing in Auntie Cath's life.

In the kitchen was a scribbled note. *Milk in fridge, biscuits in tin.* The note was unsigned but Megan recognised the spidery handwriting. It was that of Chloe, who Auntie Cath had employed at sixteen to help out at the cattery, and had remained as a fixture here ever since.

Megan filled the kettle with water

and stared out of the window, taking in the long garden lined with established fruit trees and neatly trimmed grass. A movement caught her eye and she drew her attention back to the windowsill. A jet-black cat was sat still as a statue — or, more appropriately, an ornament — so still that Megan had not noticed him at first.

'Hello, Old Man,' Megan said softly, reaching out two fingers to allow him to sniff them. He stared at her with his almond eyes, and Megan thought that they registered sorrow.

'How are you doing? Missing Auntie Cath? Me too,' she whispered. Old Man seemed to sigh, and then turned his head dejectedly back to his vigil at the window. Megan wondered if cats could get depressed, and decided she might need to look it up in one of the many books that her friend Kate had brought her for the occasion. Perhaps *How to Understand How Your Cat Really Feels* might help.

At that moment there was a crash

and urgent meowing. Megan turned to see Tinker and Belle come dashing through the cat flap. Belle went straight for Megan's legs, twisting in and out like a darting fish, whilst Tinker did a funny sort of dance that made Megan wonder if she was praying for rain.

'Nice to see that some of us are doing okay.' With one hand she tried to push Belle off, the cat having decided that clawing her way up Megan's leg was the way to go.

'I expect you want feeding?' Megan asked, half-expecting a reply. She didn't know much about cats, but she had seen enough cat food adverts on the TV to recognise the tell-tell signs.

She went straight to the cupboard where Auntie Cath kept the cat food and picked up a sachet at random, as well as a clean bowl. She ripped the top off the sachet and squeezed the contents into the bowl. Then the smell hit her. It was so strong that it practically made her eyes water. She screwed up her nose in disgust and tried to hold her breath. Placing the bowl between the two dancing felines, she watched expectantly as Tinker fell on the food and started to make what could only be described as slurping noises. Belle looked at her as if to say, 'And?' Megan tried to gently push her towards the food, and was rewarded with a side-swipe of a clawed paw. Seeking advice, Megan looked at Old Man, who simply glanced at her pityingly before return-ing to his job of staring out the window.

With no help forthcoming, Megan returned to the cat food cupboard, look-ing for inspiration, before pulling out a tin from a different box. She tugged the ring-pull and was again overwhelmed by the smell: the contents looked like fish guts, or at least fish guts that had been partially digested and vomited back up. Gagging slightly, she gingerly spooned out the contents, placed the bowl on the floor, and shoved the tin in the bin in the vain hope of reducing the powerful fish odour.

'Ah, that's sweet — giving them party

food to cheer 'em up.'

The back door closed as Chloe stepped in, wiping her boots carefully on the mat. Megan looked up and smiled before glancing back at Tinker and Belle, thinking that they did not look like they needed cheering up to her.

Megan poured hot water onto Chloe's organic white tea bag and prodded it dubiously, it didn't seem to be affected by the hot water at all — but perhaps that was why it was called white tea? She handed it over, marvelling at her beautifully manicured hands. Megan's had permanent dry patches between her fingers and closely-trimmed fingernails; the former due to the constant hand-washing, and the latter due to the more hands-on aspects of nursing.

Chloe always looked as if she was about to get changed ready for her next photo shoot. She had chocolate-brown hair tied in a knot, which somehow managed to look glamorously wind-swept. Megan knew that if she tried something similar, she would look like her hair hadn't seen a brush in three years. Chloe was slim, but with curves, and her careless dress sense seemed to only accentuate her beauty.

'So . . . ' Chloe said, sipping at her tea. Megan fought the urge to reply 'So what?' and shrugged instead.

'Mmm,' Chloe murmured.

Unable to keep communicating by non-verbal methods alone, Megan said, 'I just want to reassure you that I am going to keep the cattery — well, for the year at least. Auntie Cath wanted me to — sort of her last request, I guess — so here I am . . . '

Megan's voice trailed off. Chloe was staring at her with a child's wide-eyed fascination.

'Er, so you've no need to worry; about your job, I mean.'

Chloe continued to gaze and Megan, clearly unable to outstare this girl, turned round and made a grab for the battered biscuit tin. Tinker looked up hopefully and Megan gave him her 'Don't even think about it, buster' stare which she usually reserved for truculent junior doctors. Tinker walked off with his tail in the air and an aloof body language, very much like your average junior doctor.

'Biscuit?' she said, shoving the tin under Chloe's nose, forcing her to break her impromptu staring competition. Chloe turned her eyes to examine the biscuits as if they were diamonds. Getting inpatient now, Megan jiggled the tin.

'No, ta.'

Megan fought the urge to roll her eyes, and helped herself to a gingernut — her personal favourite. Cradling her tea in one hand and the biscuit tin in the other, feeling she would need more very soon, she made her way through to the country-cottage-style lounge, plopping herself down in the comfiest armchair. She waited expectantly, and a full minute later Chloe floated in to the lounge and sat down, looking momentarily surprised as if she had forgotten that Megan was even here.

'So, I want to get stuck in as soon as possible. Perhaps you could show me the ropes tomorrow morning?'

Chloe's face was positively vacant.

'What time do you start?' Megan asked, deciding one question at the time might be the way to go.

''Bout six; the boys and girls get impatient if the service is late.'

Megan blinked. Six wasn't so bad — she had been working shifts for years — but she was quite surprised at how much Chloe had spoken, possibly her longest sentence ever.

'Okay, that's not a problem. Is Graham around?'

Chloe tilted her head to one side and nodded slowly, almost cautiously. Megan made to get up. 'I ought to go and talk to him, make sure he understands about his job being safe.'

More staring.

'Or maybe I'll leave it till tomorrow?'

Chloe nodded sagely.

Megan sat down wondering if the OED made a Chloe Version.

3

The room was dark so Megan was reasonably sure it was still night-time. There was no light from the curtains, but she rarely slept through till morning — years of shift work had played havoc with her routine. The door to her room, which she had left ajar, squeaked as it was slowly pushed open. Megan lay still, faking sleep and trying to stop herself calling out. She had never been afraid when she had stayed with Auntie Cath, but the bungalow seemed to have an eerie feel now she was on her own. Her eyes sought helplessly in the dark for shapes that might give her an idea of who was in the room. A weight landed on her chest, and she flung it and the duvet off herself and leapt out of bed, taking up what she hoped was a fighting stance.

'Whoever you are, I know how to defend myself!' she squealed — not exactly the confident manner she'd been going for.

The darkness was total, but Megan could sense movement in the room, and it seemed to be coming from all around her. She knew that she needed light: nothing was as scary if you could see. She stumbled in what she hoped was the direction of the door, hands groping in front of her to prevent herself walking into anything. Hands didn't help as she pitched headfirst over the bin, crashing into the door, which swung back and banged into the wall. With one hand she tried to pull down her nightie, which had somehow worked its way up to her armpits, while with the other she searched for the light switch. Breathing hard and trying to psych herself up for a fight, she blinked in the sudden brightness.

The guest room, tastefully decorated in browns and creams, looked unchanged with its piles of boxes and bags; and, save for herself, completely empty. Megan quickly inspected the wardrobe for lurking axe murderers, mentally telling herself off for being such an idiot — then there it was again. The hairs on her arms and back of her neck stood to attention as her heart started to beat out a call to arms.

It's behind you! was all she could think. Grabbing a heavy ceramic (and quite possibly expensive) vase, she headed out the bedroom door. Ten minutes later — having checked every possible place that even a miniature burglar could have hidden — feeling somewhat sheepish and intensely glad that no one was here to witness this embarrassing moment, she slipped back into bed.

By the time Megan had repeated this process two more times, she was convinced that either she was losing her mind, or else should be revising her opinions on whether ghosts really existed.

★ ★ ★

Megan's alarm clock shrieked and she fell out of bed. She wasn't even certain whether she had been asleep, or just lying there and expecting it to go off any second, but somehow it had still managed to surprise her. Kneeling on the floor with the early-morning sun peeking through the window, she could not quite believe what a night she had had. This cannot go on, she told herself firmly. You need to get a grip! She imagined for a moment Auntie Cath looking down from the best seats in heaven and having a good giggle — well, at least she was proving to be amusing to someone.

Struggling to her feet, she made her way towards the shower; then, glancing back at the clock, realised that she had reset it to 5.50 in a desperate attempt at getting an hour's sleep, which meant she had no time for niceties this morning. She kicked open the lid of her suitcase and scrambled around for an old pair of jeans and a t-shirt which had seen better days. She pulled on some fresh underwear (well, even when she was late, Megan had some non-negotiable standards) and dragged a hairbrush through her shoulder-length hair. It was shiny at the top, indicating the need for a wash, and static at the ends, so she looked rather half-crazed. With an exasperated sigh she searched for a hair tie to use, but couldn't find one. She knew she had left one on her bedside cabinet last night, but now it was gone. Hearing noises outside, which had to be Chloe, she took one last miserable glance in the mirror and promised herself a long soak in a warm bath and some pampering as soon as everything in the cattery was organised.

As she passed the kettle she flicked the switch. Since she was now the boss, she thought she should decide when they got to have the first cup of coffee of the day. Three expectant feline faces looked up at her: they had formed a sort of a queue as if waiting for service in a shop.

'Morning, guys. I don't suppose you heard any ghosts and ghoulies last night, did you?'

The cats seem to have ignored her

comment; either that, or they had decided that she was completely mad and thought it best not to reply. Sighing again, she reached for food from the cat cupboard, and served up three different sorts to the fussy animals. There was the sound of sloppy eating and Megan decided that this was probably a good sign. At least she had managed to get something right on her first morning.

Grabbing her jacket and unlocking the back door she stepped outside, taking a moment to take in the peace and quiet. No traffic noise. It was bliss.

'We're going to have to call a vet, Graham, the poor boy is in a bad way!'

Megan didn't wait to hear a reply but ran to the door to the cattery pens.

'What's going on?' she gasped as she staggered through the door, 'Is one of them sick?' She looked around the ordered pens to try and work out who was in need of attention. Chloe reached out and grabbed her arm tightly.

'It's Colonel Markington. He's — well, he's having kittens!'

Chloe's face was pale and shocked, and Megan gently led her to a chair and made her sit down. This was all she needed on her first day away from nursing — a patient!

'Take a deep breath, Chloe.'

Chloe took a shuddering sigh

'And tell me exactly what has happened.'

Chloe gulped some more air.

'I came in this morning and checked on them all first, like I normally do. They don't like it if they don't all get to say good morning first.'

Megan smiled her encouraging smile, as if to say 'go on'.

'Everyone was fine but the Colonel. He was pacing like a lion and making these awful noises. I wasn't sure what was going on. Lady Markington will be so mad if anything happens to the Colonel. He's a pedigree and worth a lot of money!'

Megan left Chloe's side and walked to the first pen. The rather rotund long-haired silver tabby cat was lying on his side panting and, it had to be said, even to a human nurse did not look well. Chloe had joined her.

'Then, well, then he had *that*.' She pointed at him, and Megan could make out what looked like a soggy bundle of fluff. 'It's a miracle. I think he's had kittens!'

Megan took a moment to let this sink in.

'But how?' she asked. She knew her knowledge of felines was pretty limited, but she was fairly sure on the anatomy of boy and girl cats.

'I know, it's the strangest thing ever. Do you think we should call the papers? We could make a fortune!' Chloe added rather hopefully.

Not exactly the type of publicity we are after, Megan thought to herself.

'No,' she said firmly. 'What the Colonel needs right now is a vet, not a photoshoot. Does Auntie Cath have a vet?'

'Oh yes, Doctor Wakefield in the village. He's a very nice man and never minds if we have to take in an emergency out-of-hours. I'll call and ask if we can meet him at the surgery.'

Megan nodded, keeping one eye on the Colonel, who seemed to be panting more. She suspected that kitten number two was about to make its debut appearance.

4

Twenty minutes later, Megan, Chloe and the Colonel — plus possibly two kittens — were in the Cath's Cats van and speeding through the lanes to the veterinary clinic which was on the other side of the village. Megan was impressed that a small country vet could afford such palatial buildings, and then she caught sight of the sign. *Equine Surgery* in large bold black letters, underneath which was written *Small pets also catered for*. There was an impressive reception building which looked as if it had been the village squire's house before its conversion. It was old, with three storeys and large bay windows. To the side were several large outbuildings and parking for a range of cars, Land Rovers and horse carriers.

This was Auntie Cath's vet? Megan had a sense of impending doom.

As it turned out, she was right. She stood at the doorstep, having tugged on the bell-pull, and waited for the door to be opened.

A youngish girl in a smart green veterinary nurse's uniform answered. 'Please come through. Doctor Wakefield will be with you shortly.'

Megan, listing to one side due to the weight of the Colonel and his offspring, struggled to keep up as the nurse bustled quickly past several rooms to the right and left. Finally, she stopped outside a heavy oak door with what looked like a gold-plated name sign reading *Doctor William Wakefield*. His name was followed by a long string of letters that made no sense to Megan, but suggested that he was possibly a little overqualified to deal with a male cat that had somehow managed to have kittens.

The nurse knocked on the door and waited. There was a pause of a few seconds before a voice boomed, 'Come.'

Megan raised one eyebrow at Chloe, who looked blankly back. Perhaps this was normal for Doctor Wakefield. Taking a deep breath, and remembering all she had learnt from dealing with difficult consultants, Megan put her most professional expression on her face. She was, after all, in business now, and this was simply a business matter.

They walked into a consulting room which was large and airy, with one wide window revealing the extent of the grounds owned by the surgery. They were mostly neat lawns and rosebushes, but off to one side Megan could make out several paddocks and a large ringed-off area that she presumed was for exercising horses. The consulting room was all white and stainless steel, and seemed to have a whole range of expensive-looking equipment. Megan heaved up the cat basket and put it on the table.

'And how may I be of assistance at this fine early hour?'

Megan dragged her attention away from the view and looked into the eyes of Doctor Wakefield. He was handsome in an English-country-boy kind of way, his hair ruffled in an 'I know I am ruggedly handsome and don't have to worry' manner. He was taller than her and, she figured, a few years older. She was caught off-guard by his appearance, but in charge of her senses enough to pick up the sarcasm in his voice. She opened her mouth to speak, but had got no further than stating her name before she was interrupted.

'It's the Colonel, Doctor Wakefield — he's, well, he's had kittens! It's a miracle,' Chloe said breathlessly

Megan fought hard not to roll her eyes. This was so embarrassing, and she needed to do something to retrieve the situation. She cleared her throat.

'Chloe is right in the sense that we have had some unexpected arrivals this morning, and . . . '

Megan's voice trailed off as she caught sight of Doctor Wakefield's face. One eyebrow was raised slightly, and somehow he managed to look both bored and incredulous at the same time.

'A miracle?' he asked, slowly, as if Megan would not understand him if he spoke at normal speed.

Megan couldn't help it but she could feel herself blush.

'Well, no — not a miracle. More of a surprise, really.'

'I see. Cats do have kittens from time to time, particularly if they have not been spayed.' He looked carefully from Chloe back to Megan.

'But the Colonel's a boy, so he can't have kittens!' Chloe blurted out, seemingly oblivious to the heavily sarcastic atmosphere.

Doctor Wakefield's gaze remained firmly fixed on Megan's face, and she closed her eyes briefly, wishing she could go back to bed and start the day again. In fact, while she was at it, she might as well go back to the night before and try to get a good night's sleep.

Doctor Wakefield lifted the lid of the cat basket. 'The Colonel is, in fact, a girl; since Lady Markington does not believe in, and I quote, 'unnecessary veterinary intervention', the Colonel has not been neutered.'

Megan chewed the inside of her cheek, a habit she fell into when she was wishing she was somewhere else.

Chloe had an expression on her face as if the sun was rising.

'So the Colonel's . . . a girl?' Chloe asked

'Indeed. Might I suggest, Miss Falstaff, that perhaps you familiarise yourself with rudimentary cat physiology to avoid making such mistakes again in the future?'

He turned and washed his hands in the stainless steel sink, giving Megan enough time to remove the mortified expression from her face and replace it with her professionally blank one that she reserved for times such as this.

'Now, let's have a look at you, My Lady. Lady Markington would not be best pleased if anything were to happen to you as a result of this unnecessary visit to the vets.'

Megan held the basket as the Colonel was lifted out, and peeked in to see the two new arrivals, as well as to avoid making eye contact with the vet.

A few minutes later, after satisfying himself that neither mother nor babies were any worse for their journey, Doctor Wakefield — having ignored his human guests the whole time — returned his attention back to Megan.

'I would recommend, Miss Falstaff, that you leave the Colonel and her kittens here with me. They are in good order at present, but I would not like to guess at the impact another unnecessary trip might have upon them. Lady Markington returns the day after tomorrow, I believe. I will let her housekeeper know that the Colonel is here, and she can collect her from us when she is ready.'

Megan felt like a schoolgirl who had just received a telling-off from the head-teacher. This was not the most auspicious start to her new career. Maybe it was a good thing that Auntie Cath had only asked that she look after the business for a year before selling it. She wondered if the cattery would still be in any shape to sell after she had been in charge for that long. Taking a deep breath, she forced herself to regroup.

'Thank you for your time, Doctor Wakefield, it was much appreciated. I apologise for disturbing you so early in the morning.'

Without waiting for a reply, she walked quickly back through the surgery and out the door. She was sat in the car with her seatbelt done up before Chloe had even made it out of the building. Resisting the urge to sound the horn to get her to hurry up, she comforted herself with the thought that she would never have to see or speak to Doctor Wakefield again, especially if he was going to return the Colonel to Lady Markington. His words replayed in her head, and she cringed at the sarcasm and how foolish she must have looked. His image also popped into her mind, and she remembered his handsome face, rugged hair and keen eyes.

Stop it! she ordered herself. He might look nice but he wasn't exactly pleasant when it came to holding a conversation. And, more to the point, she had met plenty of his type before. Well-educated and condescending. Treating her and everyone else who didn't have a top university degree as if they were somehow a lesser being. She had learnt to cope with it as a nurse — she hadn't had much choice — but here it was going to be different. Here she was her own boss, for the first time ever. Here she was going to choose the people that she spent time with, and there was no way the haughty Doctor William Wakefield was going to be one of them.

5

'Have you seen this?'

Megan blinked in surprise as Chloe shoved a newspaper under her nose. She sighed and put down her coffee. She had finished helping Chloe clean out all the cats, and had been looking forward to a quiet hour before they officially opened on her second day in charge.

'Er, no. Should I have?' Megan asked

She looked up expectantly, but Chloe didn't step in with an explanation, even when Megan raised a questioning eyebrow. She sighed and picked up the folded paper. She unfolded it, picked up her coffee, and took a sip. As it happened, this turned out to be a big mistake — a second later she sprayed the kitchen counter with freshly-ground expensive coffee. She coughed to try and clear her throat from the half-swallowed liquid that remained in her mouth. She twitched the newspaper so that she could see all of the front page.

CATH'S CATS' CATASTROPHIC MISTAKE!

Megan's eyes opened even wider as she read the article that was front-page news for the *Little River Courier*.

Our intrepid reporter has uncovered serious errors and mismanagement from the new owners of Cath's Cats. As our regular readers will know, the previous proprietor of the cattery, Cathleen Somers, was a well-respected and well-known resident of Little River. She was known for her intelligent understanding of all things feline, and trusted by many of our readers to care for their beloved cats, who for some are more like family than many human relatives.

The new manager of Cath's Cats is a Miss Megan Fulstaff, an unknown but presumably distant relative of

Ms Somers, who appears to have inherited the business but alas appears to have none of the acumen with regards to the business of cats.

Miss Fulstaff had only been in residence for one day when a feline emergency struck one of the most important residents. Colonel Markington, the four-year-old Persian pedigree of our very own Lady Markington was rushed to the Wakefield Veterinary Surgery for immediate attention. *What emergency had befallen this poor feline?* I hear you ask. Well, the Colonel was thought to be the cause of a miraculous event — the birth of kittens. This may not seem to be such a remarkable occurrence to our readers, who will of course know that such events, whilst a cause of celebration, could hardly be considered to be miraculous.

Unfortunately, for a person with Miss Fulstaff's understanding, this would indeed appear to be a miracle . . . and why? Miss Fulstaff believed that the Colonel was a boy. Yes, that would indeed be a miracle — however, one would hope that the owner of a cattery would know enough to tell the difference between a male and female cat!

A source at the veterinary clinic is quoted as saying, 'It was unusual to attend the surgery that early in the morning for something which would not be considered an emergency by any average person. The cat in question was managing well with her kittens and was having no apparent difficulties. In fact, to move a cat at this sensitive stage of delivery was possibly the most harmful aspect of the case.'

We are also led to believe that Miss Fulstaff intended to try and sell her story to a well-known national newspaper, and we can only surmise that she is in the business purely to make a quick buck. It remains to be seen whether the business will thrive under Miss Fulstaff's care, but we can only hope that she undertakes some course of study to improve her knowledge of our feline friends.

Megan searched for the name of the reporter. She needed to know who had written such an unfair report, and also possibly to point out that they ought to get their facts right — like how to spell her name correctly.

Abigail Curan was the culprit. She scanned the headlines again and took a deep breath. How was giving this woman a piece of her mind going to achieve anything other than to give her more fodder for her newspaper? The chances were that if Megan lost her temper with her, Abigail would write that she was a crazy lunatic who was a danger to society.

She sipped at her coffee and screwed up her face when she realised that it had gone cold. She pushed back her stool and threw the remainder down the sink. Old Man was in his usual position of staring out the window in miserable silence. She stroked him gently between the ears.

'Well, Old Man, not the most auspicious start. I wonder what Auntie Cath would say if she was here right now.'

Old Man turned to her with mournful eyes and an expression which said: 'Well, she's not, kid, so you'll just have to try and make it on your own like the rest of us.' He snuffled once and returned to studying the garden.

Something moved behind her and she turned swiftly, her heart racing up a notch. But it was only Chloe, who Megan had forgotten was there. Chloe was cradling Belle, and seemed to be whispering in her ear.

'Well it could have been worse?' Megan said out loud, hoping for some words of comfort.

'Cath was in the newspaper once,' Chloe said in a faraway voice.

'Really?' Megan said hopefully. She waited, but as usual Chloe did not pick up on the verbal cue that she was expected to answer. Gritting her teeth and trying not to lose her temper, which now felt unusually short, she asked, 'What was she in the paper for?' Working on the principle that with Chloe, a direct, to-the-point question was probably best.

Chloe looked at her with her head on one side. 'She won an award, didn't she, Belley-Boo?'

Megan's hope faded. 'What kind of award?'

Chloe beckoned with her head and stepped out of the back door. Megan followed her down the concrete path and into the bungalow extension that contained the cattery office. Chloe settled herself into one of the guest armchairs and proceeded to brush Belle's already glossy coat. Megan glared at her in frustration, and was about to tell Chloe exactly what she thought of her lack of communication skills, when her eyes caught sight of a certificate in a frame which was separate from the certificates of insurance.

'*Little River Courier* Small Business of the Year 2015. Cath's Cattery.'

Megan sat herself in the chair behind the large wooden desk. Auntie Cath had won a business award just last year. She shook her head; she had been in charge for all of twenty-four hours, and they had already been headline news in the local newspaper. What was Auntie Cath thinking? Leaving her a cattery to run for a year — this was her idea of giving her a fresh start?

She was shaken from her self-pity by the noise of the phone ringing. She looked to Chloe, who was engrossed in brushing Belle and clearly had no intention of answering the phone. Megan rolled her eyes and lifted the receiver.

'Hello, Cath's Cats. Megan speaking. How may I help you?'

'Is that Megan Fulstaff?'

'Well, it's Falstaff actually; but yes, it is.' Megan rolled her eyes again.

'Oh, I see. Well, I was supposed to bring my cat Archibald in today, but I'm afraid I will have to cancel.'

Megan reached for the diary in which all the bookings were kept, all the while thinking that they really ought to be computerised by now.

'Oh, I see. A change of plans, Mrs. Golding?' she asked politely.

There were a few seconds of silence at the other end, then the sound of a throat being cleared.

'Well, no dear, not exactly. It's just — well, if I might be honest, I am concerned about leaving dear Archibald in your establishment.'

Megan groaned inwardly. Clearly the *Little River Courier* was well-read.

'I understand your concerns, Mrs. Golding, and I appreciate that this morning's newspaper report probably has raised some issues for you; but it was an honest mistake, and perhaps you can understand that my only concern was for the Colonel's wellbeing.' And if I had managed to get a decent night's sleep, I probably would have handled it differently, she thought to herself.

'Oh dear, I don't mean to be harsh. It must be very difficult taking over from Cathleen. It's just — well, she had a way with Archibald. She was so good with cats; God rest her soul. We do miss her so much, I'm sure that Archibald has been quite down in the mouth since I told him. He is such a delicate individual, and feels things quite keenly, you know.'

'I miss Cathleen very much, and you are right — she definitely had a way with all things feline. I hope that I have learnt a little of what she knew from all the time I spent with her as a child and later.'

'Please don't think me insensitive. I know that Cathleen was very fond of you. She spoke of you often, you know: she was very proud of you, and frequently said that you were the nearest to a family of her own that she ever got.'

Megan swallowed the lump that appeared in her throat. She wished Auntie Cath was here — she would know what to do — and Megan could almost imagine her arms around her in a bear hug and kissing her on the top of her head. She wrapped one arm around herself and concentrated on avoiding the onslaught of tears that threatened to flow.

'And now I've upset you. I'm so sorry, but listen — I will bring Archibald in. After all, I trusted Cathleen; and, well, I guess you are the next best thing.'

Megan forced a smile and hoped it showed in her voice.

'That's wonderful. I believe that you wanted to bring Archibald in at two o'clock?'

'That's right. Arthur and I will drop him off on the way to our son's in Kensington.'

'Then I will see you then.'

'Goodbye, dear.'

'Goodbye, Mrs. Golding.'

Megan hung up the phone, feeling pleased with herself. She had a way with people; her years as a nurse had taught her that. Surely it would be a simple case of applying the same principles to her feline charges . . . wouldn't it?

6

The feeling did not last long. In the course of the morning they had three cancellations, none of whom could be persuaded to change their minds, and two early pick-ups. Megan had fought the urge to charge them for the full length of time — being churlish was probably not going to win their business back. Instead, she opted for her best nursing tone, apologetic and yet friendly, offering a reduced rate for their next visit should they chose to come again.

The doorbell sounded and Megan walked around to the side gate. She slipped the latch and pulled it open.

A tall man stood holding a wicker cat basket; from the way it rocked from side to side, Megan could tell it was occupied. The man had deep eyes, a sort of grey-green that seemed to draw attention to themselves. He was tall, maybe six feet, and muscly without the pumped-up look. He was gazing at her in much the same way that she was looking at him, but thankfully Megan came to her senses first.

'Hi there, I'm Megan, and I assume you have a guest for us?' She directed her gaze to the cat basket, which continued to swing despite his firm grip.

He looked startled for a moment.

'Er, yes, that's right. I've brought Ernie in for his usual holiday. You know, a week in a luxury hotel being waited on hand and foot.'

'Well, he's come to the right place.' Megan smiled and unlatched the door holding it open for the tall man to step through.

'Greg Ford,' he said, with one arm outstretched as if to shake her hand; but at that moment Ernie, furious at being caged, let out a deep grumbling howl, and the basket rocked so much that Greg had to use both hands to prevent it falling to the floor. Megan smiled and tried to push down her rising anxiety at the unruly feline, gesturing to Greg to follow her.

They walked down to the cattery office. Megan opened the door and was a little relieved that Chloe seemed to have disappeared, meaning that she had this handsome man all to herself. She smiled to herself, thinking of the conversation she had had with Kate before she left. Forty-eight hours after arrival, and she had already met one man with some potential — at least in the looks department, at any rate!

Megan flicked open the diary. 'Well, Ernie is going to be in pen eleven — it's the corner one at the end, best view of the garden.' She smiled, and was rewarded with a wide grin and a flash of very white and very straight teeth — you had to love a man who looked after his teeth.

'Shall we get him settled, and then we can run through the paperwork? I don't think he's over-keen on his mode of transportation.'

'You're telling me! You should see how much fun it is trying to coax him in in the first place! Let's just say I have to allow at least a one-hour window, or else I would miss my flight.'

Megan dangled the keys which locked the pens, and let her and her guests into the first compartment. Closing the door carefully behind them to avoid any other guests escaping, she opened the second door and stepped through. The guests were seemingly restless — they were greeted by a pitched caterwauling, which seemed to increase in volume the further down the run they walked.

'Are they always this noisy?'

' 'Fraid so; it's a bit of a Pavlov's dogs scenario. They see you, and they think one of four things: time to eat, time to stretch the legs, time to go home, or time to welcome a new guest. My assistant Chloe thinks that the meowing changes depending on what is going on, but personally I can't tell the difference.'

'Sounds like a wall of noise to me. Does it drive you mad?'

'I'm not sure I've been here long enough to tell, to be honest!'

Megan opened the last pen and checked that the heating in the cat house was on. Greg put the wicker basket down and opened its door. Ernie was clearly not going to play ball, because he remained sulkily inside, and gave no sign that he was intending to vacate any time soon.

'Honestly! He makes such a fuss about going in, and then won't come out when you want him to!' Greg tried shuffling the basket a little, but other than a deep-throated growl there was no change.

'I expect he'll come out when he's ready. You can leave the basket if you like — we have a storage facility, and it means you won't have to leave it in your car at the airport.'

Megan stood to one side as Greg stepped out of the pen. She shut the door and pulled the bolt firmly across.

There were not going to be any more disasters if she had anything to do with it!

'So you haven't been here long, then?'

Megan's puzzled expression seemed to register with Greg.

'You said that you hadn't been here long enough to know whether the caterwauling was going to get to you or not?' he prompted

'Oh,' she answered, studying his face to see if he was winding her up. She was certain that everyone in the village had read the newspaper, or at least heard the gossip that it had no doubt generated. But Greg's face was open and inquisitive, with no trace of sarcasm or wind-up — none that Megan could detect, anyway, and she usually had quite a good sense of what people were really about. She relaxed and grinned sheepishly.

'I've only be in charge for a couple of days. But don't worry, I'm a nurse, so I have a fair amount of common sense.'

She thought she could detect a fleeting look of concern or panic cross his face. She rested one hand on his arm in a gesture of reassurance that she used to reserve for concerned relatives of the sick.

'Don't worry. Ernie will be fine in our care. Chloe, my assistant, has been working at the cattery for years, and she is somewhat of a cat whisperer . . . like the dog whisperer, but with cats.' She grinned hopefully at her rather lame joke, and was relieved when she was rewarded by a wry smile.

'I have complete faith in your abilities, Megan. But I do have one question for you,' he said as he joined her back in the office and folded into the armchair opposite the desk.

'I was wondering if you fancied a drink with me tonight. The local pub's not bad, if you ignore the yokels.'

Megan frowned a little.

'I thought you were supposed to be flying out tonight?' she asked playfully. Now it was Greg's turn to blush a little, the colour rising quickly from his cheeks to his eyes.

'Well, yes, but it's a business trip; and let's just say that for the right reason I could delay my departure . . . what do you think?'

Megan's insides felt like they had turned to mush, and her heart was beating alarmingly fast. It had been a while since a handsome, available guy had asked her out. She quickly scanned his left hand, and was relieved to see that, other than a plain silver band on his middle finger, it was ring-less, and there was no tell-tale tan mark on his wedding finger to show that one had recently been in residence.

'Well, I suppose so, as long as I'm not going to get you into trouble with your boss?' Megan busied herself completing some contact information on Ernie's record card as she studied Greg from underneath her lashes.

'Well, my boss is pretty reasonable, and I'm sure if he met you he would completely understand.'

Megan shook her head in disbelief at his terrible line. He shrugged unselfconsciously.

'Let me guess — you work for yourself,' she said ruefully.

'Yeah, I do; and the good news is, I'm pretty lenient with my employees. I'll swing by about seven — the food's not bad, so maybe we could grab a bite to eat as well?' he added hopefully.

Megan studied his eager face for a moment. Yup, her internal sensors were sending her all positive messages.

'Sure, why not?' Struggling to keep her face composed.

'Good, then; see you later.' And with that, Greg was gone. Megan watched him walk back down the path and disappear through the gate. She waited a full five minutes, timing it by the ticking clock on the office wall, before she let herself get excited. It would not be good if he saw her jump around in excitement.

She was still dancing just a little and whooping when the door opened and an older man with thinning grey hair stepped into the office. Megan dropped her dancing hands to her sides and pretended to busily study the diary for the other guests she would be expecting throughout the day. Unfortunately, all the supposed guests had cancelled — or, at least, their owners had. In Megan's experience, when caught out like this, it was best to take the time to compose oneself and then just act like nothing unusual had happened.

'Hello Graham, I have been waiting to speak to you, but I haven't seen much of you since I arrived.' She smiled in what she hoped was a reassuring but boss-like manner.

Graham rewarded her with a scowl.

'Been busy working,' he growled

'Of course. I just wanted to let you know that your job is safe, in the short term anyway. I intend to honour Cathleen's request and run the cattery for the year — and who knows, if I like it and it likes me, I might stay on.' Her mind wandered to the mental photograph of Greg that she had taken — quite possibly she would have another reason to stay now.

Graham was grumbling something under his breath, and from his body language Megan was pretty sure that it wasn't words of encouragement.

'Sorry, Graham, I didn't quite catch what you said?' she asked mildly in her best schoolteacher's voice that she used to use on medical students.

Graham scowled and shuffled his feet on the floor, with more mumbling. Megan could not quite believe that Auntie Cath, who could talk the hind legs of the proverbial donkey, could employ two almost mute members of staff — or maybe that was it, she liked to have the floor entirely to herself.

'Do you have any questions?' she asked, not expecting to get a response, and she was right ... just more mumbling and shuffling.

'Right then, if there is nothing else, I have some more unpacking to do.' She shut the diary firmly and looked at him with one eyebrow raised. He looked up for a moment and then shuffled out.

Megan sighed; it didn't matter where you worked, but managing people was always the hardest part of any job. She forced the thought of her interesting staff from her mind. She had some unpacking to do — somewhere in the pile of boxes and suitcases was a smart yet casual outfit that she hoped was perfect for a first date at the local pub.

7

Megan took one last pass at her lip gloss and studied her reflection in the mirror. She had brushed her hair out, aiming for the slightly-tousled-but-relaxed look — she wasn't convinced that she had pulled it off, but considering she had spent the last ten working years wearing her hair in a military-style bun, she couldn't expect her hair styling gene to switch back on after only forty-eight hours. She was wearing her favourite leather jacket, which was dark brown and fitted her curves — courtesy of her last shopping trip with Kate. She had opted for her best blue jeans and black boots and a plain black t-shirt. She grabbed her matching brown bag, quietly thanking Kate for insisting that she buy appropriate accessories. One last look in the mirror and she realised she had company.

'What do you think, guys? Am I dressed for a first date?' Belle and Tinker sat one on each side of her with heads cocked to the side. Tinker seemed to shrug, and turned around to wash his back. Belle sniffed at Megan's leg and meowed, which she decided was a positive sign — although she did try one last squirt of perfume just to make sure that she smelled good, and not of cats.

Megan couldn't believe her new life had taken such a positive turn so fast. When she had decided to follow Auntie Cath's last wish, to walk away from her old life and try a new one, she had been doubtful that anything would truly change. Her old life was basically all about work: nursing had the power to do that to you. Whilst she loved her job, loved caring for people, it took most of her emotional energy, and left very little of that to spend on herself. She had friends, of course, like Kate, who she managed to see from time to time when her shifts allowed; but there wasn't much time for Megan to figure out what she want from her life — other than when she might finally catch up on the sleep her shift pattern deprived her of.

Megan took one last glance at herself in the long mirror, and raised a hand to tousle her hair one final time. She had to admit she had butterflies in her stomach at the thought of her date. Of course, it wasn't really a *date*, she told herself firmly — Greg was probably just being friendly to the newcomer — but it still gave her a little fizz of excitement. Auntie Cath had been the wisest person that Megan had ever known, and it seemed that it was right. It was always possible that Auntie Cath had met Greg before and decided that he was the one. Despite being single herself, Auntie Cath had an excellent eye for love, which she had told Megan was due to her love of reading all things romance.

Megan shook herself; she was getting way ahead. This was just dinner with a man she had just met, so mentally planning their life together was not the way to approach this!

'Be cool, be casual,' she told herself as she walked into the kitchen.

Old Man was sat in his usual spot on the kitchen windowsill. He turned towards her and looked her up and down, like a parent checking on the suitability of their child's outfit. He sniffed and then meowed. Megan reached over and gently scratched him in his favourite spot behind his ears; to her surprise he purred, for the first time since she had arrived. Megan smiled.

'I take it you approve, Old Man. I'll tell you all about it when I get home. Maybe we'll even open a tin of tuna to celebrate.'

Megan thought she could see a sparkle in Old Man's eyes, which made her giggle. It was doubtful he was looking forward to a gushing retelling of her first date in years — more likely it was the thought of tuna — but still. If you lived with cats, you had to take all the encouragement you could get.

When the doorbell sounded, Megan

jumped, which was ridiculous since she knew that Greg was coming to pick her up. She made herself count to ten so as not to appear too eager, and then walked in to the hall to open the door.

'Wow,' Greg said, and Megan could feel a pleased embarrassment colour her cheeks. In his hand he had a small bunch of sweet pea flowers, which were Megan's favourite, and again she wondered if Auntie Cath had managed to have some kind of hand in this. Greg blinked, then seemed to remember where he was and what he was holding. He held out his hand.

'These are for you,' he said, and Megan took them from him before stepping back away from the door.

'They're beautiful, thank you. Come in for a minute while I put them in water?' And she led the way to the back of the bungalow and into the kitchen.

'Cath's inner sanctum,' he said softly, as if in awe. 'I don't think any of the other villagers have ever been allowed in here.'

Megan laughed so as not to allow the grief back in at that moment.

'That sounds like Auntie Cath,' she said, remembering how fiercely Cath had protected her privacy. She obviously hadn't managed to keep her tone as light as she hoped, for she felt Greg reach out a hand for her arm.

'I'm sorry,' he said, and sounded it. 'It must all be pretty raw, and I expect you don't need an idiot like me reminding you of it.'

Megan swallowed and then turned to face him.

'It's fine,' she said. 'Actually, I like to talk about her sometimes, and it's nice when the other person actually knew her. Most of my friends in London never got to meet her.' Greg smiled at her, and it was so warm and understanding that she thought she might dissolve into tears and throw herself in to his arms right there and then. Only Old Man's stare made her control herself.

'Why don't we head out? We can get something to eat, and then have a stroll around the village? I can show you all the sights that Little River has to offer, so that will take all of five minutes.'

Megan laughed, and this time it wasn't because she was trying to hold back a tide of emotion.

A short drive, and they arrived at the Markington Arms. Megan couldn't help but raise an eyebrow at the name.

'Oh yes,' Greg said, seeing her expression, 'the former lady of the manor has her claws in everywhere. She campaigned for years to get the pub to change its name, and the locals eventually gave in. Of course, everyone still calls it the King's Head, but don't tell Lady Markington.' His eyes twinkled mischievously.

'I wouldn't dream of it,' Megan said stepping out of the car. 'I haven't met her yet, but I anticipate an awkward first encounter after the whole feline debacle.'

Greg walked with Megan up to the front door of the pub. It was a classic country pub with a thatched roof and white walls. The windows were small and criss-crossed with lead.

'I heard something about that on the old village rumour mill. You'll have to tell me all the details over dinner.'

Megan rolled her eyes. Sharing a mortifyingly embarrassing moment with a new guy who she had just met and was already starting to like was not necessarily a good idea. But at least he had a sense of humour, and would no doubt have a good laugh when she told him exactly what had happened.

They walked in to the main bar of the pub. Although it was a fairly warm autumn night, the two log fires at each end were lit, and made the pub feel especially cosy.

Greg spotted a table for two near one of the fires and led the way over.

'What would you like to drink?'

'White wine spritzer, please,' Megan said, noting the look of surprise on his face. She wasn't a big drinker, and had no intention of starting tonight when the consequences might be embarrassing.

Megan watched as Greg walked to the bar. He greeted the people sat on stools there like old friends, so this was clearly his local. She leaned back in her chair and took in her surroundings. The pub was busy, with most tables full of couples or groups, and it was a relaxed, friendly atmosphere. When she met people's eyes they smiled at her — which was a bit of shock after years of living in London, where you perfected the art of pretending you couldn't see the other six million people who lived there.

Megan could feel herself relax a little. Perhaps she could make a life for herself here. She smiled to herself and looked towards the other end of the pub. The face sat in the mirror image of her chair did not smile. In fact, it was a look filled with dislike — and, if Megan didn't know better, hate. She blinked and fought to keep her expression neutral. She was looking into the stormy face of Doctor William Wakefield, Little River's vet.

8

'You okay?' a voice asked, and a wine glass was waved in front of her face.

Megan managed a smile. 'Fine,' she said looking up in to Greg's expression of concern.

'Are you sure? You look like you've just seen a ghost or something.'

Megan took a sip of her wine to give her a few moments to process what had just happened. She knew she had made an idiot of herself at Doctor Wakefield's surgery that morning, and that he was less than impressed with her knowledge of cats, but she could think of nothing which would warrant that level of dislike.

'No ghosts,' Megan said. 'At least, not here.' Greg looked puzzled and Megan laughed thinking she should really tell him that story and avoid talking about what had just happened. She wondered if she had imagined it. Greg scanned the room and Megan watched as his eyes became fixed on Doctor Wakefield's ramrod-straight back.

'Ah,' Greg said, turning back to Megan. 'The aloof and pompous Doctor Wakefield, I presume?'

Megan sighed.

'It would seem I didn't make a very good first impression.'

Greg laughed, but it was brittle, with no humour.

'Megan, believe me when I tell you that no one does. In fact, no mere mortal could ever meet the exacting standards of His Royal Highness.'

Greg did a mock bow, seated in his chair, and Megan laughed. If that was what Wakefield was like with everyone, then there was no point worrying about it. She had met doctors like him in her time, and it didn't matter what you did, you could never alter their opinion so it was a waste of effort to try.

'Why do I feel like there is a story there?' Megan asked, feeling her curiosity bubble up.

'It's not a very interesting one, I'm afraid. You know the sort — private school, Cambridge University, and a top vet to the horsey stars of the neighbourhood. He only got permission to set up the clinic if he agreed to deal with the lower classes' small pets as well. I don't think he has ever recovered from the shame.'

Now they both laughed, although Megan could feel her conscious pricking at her a little. She was making a judgement about Doctor Wakefield on very little information, and she usually like to take her time to come to her own conclusions.

'Anyway,' Greg said, and Megan wondered if he had read her mind, 'enough of boring conversations. You said something about ghosts?'

Once they had ordered their food and started to eat, Megan knew that she couldn't put it off any longer. She was going to have to tell him about her ghost problem.

'So?' Greg said, letting the word hang in the air.

'So,' Megan replied, 'my first night in the bungalow, and I kept waking up.'

Greg nodded to show he was listening. 'Okay, but that's not unusual for your first night in a new place?'

Megan rolled her eyes as if to say 'Give me a chance!' and Greg held up his hands to indicate his surrender.

'I didn't just *wake* up; I was *woken* up. By noises in the bedroom. Things being knocked over. And I had that feeling . . . '

Greg didn't say anything but simply raised an eyebrow, which Megan took as a sign she should continue with her story.

'The feeling like someone was there, in the bedroom with me. Staring at me.' The words came out in a jumbled rush, since she knew that if she thought about it too long she would chicken out. She half-looked up, expecting Greg to at least be grinning — or, worse, laughing — at her, but he was just studying her with a look of genuine concern.

'I got up and put the lights on,' Megan continued, since he had said nothing, 'And there was nothing there, or at least no one there.' Megan frowned again at the memory. It had happened on the first night but not the second, and she couldn't help but wonder if it would happen again tonight. She shuddered at the thought and felt a hand reach out and cover hers. She looked up and Greg gave her hand a squeeze.

'So, no obvious explanation,' he said seriously. Megan shook her head, not quite believing that she had said all that out loud to a man she had just met.

'I mean, I don't actually believe in ghosts, but I can't explain it.'

Greg opened his mouth to speak and then closed it again. Megan could tell from his expression what he was going to ask, and also the reason he hadn't actually said the words out loud.

'No, I don't think it was Auntie Cath,' she said with a smile. 'Even if I did believe something like that could happen. Her being a ghost, I mean. I can't imagine she would ever crash about knocking things over — not her style.'

'Maybe you were just having bad dreams,' Greg said thoughtfully. 'I've had a few in my time which have woken me up with a start, and I felt like they were real, but when I turned on the light . . . ' He shrugged to indicate that nothing had been there.

And with that, the conversation moved on to other subjects.

* * *

Greg pulled his car up onto the drive in front of Auntie Cath's bungalow. *My bungalow*, Megan tried to remind herself, all the while knowing that it would never be anything other than Auntie Cath's.

'I had a lovely time tonight,' Greg said, smiling at her in the dim light from the outside porch light.

'Me too,' Megan said

'I really do have to go off and do the business thing tomorrow. My boss is fair, but he also has to pay his mortgage.'

Megan laughed. They had laughed a lot during the evening, and it felt good.

'I understand. We'll take good care of Ernie for you.'

Greg nodded. 'Perhaps we could do this again? When I get back?'

'I'd like that,' Megan said. For a moment she wondered if he was going to lean in and kiss her, but something seemed to cross his face, and he smiled at her softly instead.

'That's a date, then,' he said, and Megan could feel the warm glow of excitement well up inside her.

Once indoors, she curled up in bed with a book. She hadn't brought any with her, so had selected one at random from Auntie Cath's well-laden book-shelves. With only the small bedside light on, the room was semi-dark but tonight it felt cosy rather than a place where a person could lurk unseen, as it had the previous night. Megan felt occasional bubbles of excitement rise through her as her mind wandered from her evening to Greg to the romance that she was reading.

At first, in the silence, Megan thought it was her imagination. It sounded like a tapping noise coming from the walls. Megan frowned and shivered a little, remembering her conversation earlier with Greg. No, she told herself firmly, there was no such thing as ghosts. Almost before she could complete the thought, the door suddenly started to vibrate violently. Megan froze, as if her staying still would be the only way to keep whatever it was away from her. She stared at the door, determined to convince herself that she had an overactive imagination . . . but that was when the door handle itself started to rattle.

Megan had to fight the urge to bury herself under her covers as she had done as a little girl when she was afraid of something. Instead, she gripped the duvet tightly in one hand, and then scanned the room for something she could use to defend herself. On the old-fashioned dressing table was a small cat statue — one of Auntie Cath's many trinkets. Megan knew that this one was cast in bronze, so would be very heavy. She slipped her legs out of bed and started to move towards the dressing table, wincing when she stepped on a squeaky floorboard. She paused, but all she could hear was her breath, which was coming quick and fast, like she had just run a marathon. The door was exactly as she had left it, closed, and there was silence.

She tried to tell herself it was her imagination, but she knew that wasn't true. Something was behind the door to her bedroom, and she was going to find out who — or, a small voice in her head added, *what*. But she pushed that last thought firmly aside. There were plenty of possible explanations. Graham, playing a trick, or even Chloe. An image of the pair filled her mind: neither of them seemed to have any hint of joker in their personality.

She lifted the heavy bronze — a statue of a cat sitting with its paws tucked neatly underneath — and gripped it tightly. It felt heavy and cold in her hands, but she felt better for having it near her. She took a step towards the door.

The door rattled again, as if someone were pushing against it but making no effort to pull on the handle. She took another step. Now the handle was rattling up and down once more. One thing was for certain, Megan thought; whoever was playing tricks on her was about to get an earful. She reached out her free hand, grabbed the door handle, and yanked the door open before she could change her mind. She had the bronze in her other hand, half-raised, just in case she was about to come face to face with the most incompetent burglar ever.

9

The door swung back and bounced off the wall, the noise sounding loud in her ears. Megan peered out into the hall but could see no sign of anyone, which she decided was almost worse than coming face to face with a stranger in your house in the middle of the night.

'Auntie Cath?' she whispered, feeling ridiculous but beginning to wonder what other explanation there could be.

A movement behind her made her spin on the spot — and that was when she saw it, dangling from the door handle. There was a protesting yowl, and Megan lost her grip on the heavy bronze. Before she could move out of the way it hit the floor, catching two of her toes on the way down. For a moment there was no pain, and then it felt like she had trodden on a pincushion. Now it was her turn to howl as she hopped around on one foot with her eyes watering.

'Tinker!' she yelled between sharp intakes of breath. 'What are you doing?'

Tinker, for her part, just meowed as she swung back and forth on the door handle. Megan knew she should have felt relief that she had discovered her 'ghost', but the pain in her foot was drowning out all other thoughts. She limped off in the direction of the kitchen, pressed the light switch, and then staggered over to the freezer. She pulled out a bag of frozen peas and a tea towel and then collapsed into a handy chair. Wrapping the bag of peas in the tea towel, she gingerly pressed it to her foot, which was already starting to show a bruise. She leaned back in the chair and let the slight relief from the cold wash over her.

This time she didn't jump when something heavy landed in her lap, she just opened one eye to see which of the cats it was. It was Belle, who was now headbutting her chin, and Megan couldn't help wonder if she was a partner to Tinker's crime.

Then Tinker herself wandered in, tail upright and swishing slightly at the tip. She greeted her audience with a chirp.

'It's alright for you,' Megan grumbled. 'You're lucky I didn't drop the bronze on *your* foot! If I had, I doubt you would be acting oh-so-casual now.'

Tinker chirruped again and casually sloped off to the cat flap, escaping before Megan could scold her any more. The pain in her toes was less insistent now, so she decided to take a look. All three of the middle toes on her right foot were red and swollen, and Megan sighed. They could be broken, but there was not much point going to hospital, even if she could manage to drive with her injured foot. They wouldn't do anything for her there that she couldn't do at home. Tomorrow she would strap them up, but for now all she could do was swallow a couple of paracetamol and elevate her foot.

She limped back to the bed, re-arranged her pillows so that her right foot was supported, and then slumped back on the pillows. She left the door open, hoping to avoid any more ghostly attempts by the cats to scare her into another bad night's sleep.

* * *

Megan's phone beeped and she reached for it, taking her painful foot with her as she rolled over. She winced as she remembered what had happened during the night. A quick glance at her three purple toes and the spot on the dresser where the bronze sitting cat used to be told her that it had all been real. Blearily looking at the phone, she could see she had a message, and it was from Greg.

Up early to catch my flight. Had a good time hanging out last night. Hope we can do it again soon? Any more ghost issues?

Megan fell back on the pillow and groaned. She was glad that she had figured out the mystery, but didn't looking forward to telling the tale, which she

knew made her sound like a ridicu-
lously silly person. She heard the letterbox
clank with the morning newspaper, and
then all she could think about was a
coffee so she decided to get up. She
hobbled down the hall, whilst Tinker
and Belle did their best to trip her up.
Clearly they had decided since she was
up it must be time for breakfast. With
the paper under one arm, she reached
down and stroked them.

'Just let me put the kettle on, kids.
Then I'll get your breakfast.' She smiled
at the thought she had already started
to talking to the cats, just like Auntie
Cath. The next thing she knew she
would be expecting them to answer her.
With the sound of sloppy eaters ringing
in her ears, Megan took her first sip of
coffee and unfolded the paper.

The headline made her spit out her
coffee, splattering the front page. She
coughed and spluttered but couldn't
take her eyes off the headline piece of
local news.

IS *CATH'S CATS* **HAUNTED?**

We have been made aware of complaints of ghostly goings-on in Cath's Cats, once Little River's premier hotel for your feline companions. A source states that mysterious sounds such as knocking and banging have been reported, but with no obvious cause. Doors have opened by themselves, and one source states that footsteps have been heard, accompanied by the groaning of a woman in distress. Could this be the ghost of much-loved Little River resident Cathleen Somers? Is she pacing and wringing her hands at what has become of her much-treasured business? One thing is for certain: research shows that cats are well-tuned-in to all things spiritual so it is certain that few of the remaining feline guests have been getting a good night's sleep. Have you recently used the facilities at Cath's Cats? Do you have a story to tell?

Please contact the paper at our usual number.

Having read the piece three times, Megan tossed the paper onto the kitchen table. Were newsworthy stories in this village so hard to come by that reporters for the *Little River Gazette* had to make up nonsense? She snorted in disgust — but then a thought struck her. It wasn't exactly made up. She had spoken to three people about the strange happenings in the bungalow, and one of them must have gone to the press.

Megan took another sip of coffee. Chloe had suggested they call the national newspapers when Colonel Markington had had his kittens. Maybe Chloe had spoken to the reporter. She sighed. Chloe didn't have a malicious bone in her body, but she wasn't exactly switched on to worldly matters, and she was just the sort of person a suave reporter could take advantage of.

Megan leant back in the chair and

stared at the ceiling. This could mean only one thing. She was going to have to try and have a sensible conversation with Chloe, and that was never an easy task.

10

Megan had strapped up her toes and managed to find a surgical boot that Auntie Cath had used after a bunion operation. She looked ridiculous with it on, but it was the only thing she could wear on her foot that didn't make her eyes water with pain, and working in a cattery meant that a bare foot simply wasn't an option. Looking ridiculous wasn't the only problem: it also made her waddle somewhat like a duck.

'It's not like you are going to meet anyone important,' she told herself as she looked in the mirror to tie back her hair. 'Greg is away, and Chloe and Graham don't care.'

She tried to look determined, but she could feel her face drop a little. It was hard to face the day when your new business had been dragged through the mud by the local paper two days running, and when you had to wear a surgical boot that made you walk like a waterfowl. She glared at herself one more time, her own way of telling herself to get a grip, then stumped out of the back door, down the garden, and into the little cattery office. Chloe was already there, measuring out dried cat food into a range of different bowls.

'Morning,' Megan said, thinking that with Chloe, this was as good a place as any to start.

'Morning Megan,' Chloe said, turning to her with a broad grin. 'How are you today?'

Megan stared, wondering if Chloe was trying to wind her up. It had taken quite an effort to walk up the steps into the office, and it seemed highly unlikely that even someone as away with the fairies as Chloe had failed to notice.

'Well, I hurt my foot,' Megan replied, not knowing what else to say.

'Did you? Where?' Chloe asked, eyes wide in what Megan could only assume was surprise. Megan pointed at her surgical boot, which Chloe stared at for a beat before looking up at her again, confusion marring her features.

'I dropped one of Auntie Cath's ornaments on it.'

'Why did you do that?' Chloe asked curiously.

'I didn't mean to, of course,' Megan said, wondering once again if she had accidentally started to talk in a different language. Chloe nodded.

'So I have to wear this stupid thing,' Megan continued, gesturing at her foot.

Again, Chloe looked blank.

'It's a surgical boot.'

Understanding seemed to dawn on Chloe like the sun rising in the morning.

'I did wonder that your shoes didn't match, but I figured it was a London fashion thing,' Chloe said before turning back to her task at hand. Now it was Megan's turn to stare. She blinked and remembered what she needed to speak to Chloe about.

'Have you seen the paper this

morning?' Megan asked, trying to sound casual. Chloe shook her head.

'Not yet; any good news?'

'You tell me,' Megan said wondering if Chloe would be one of those people to fold as soon as they knew the other person was on to them.

'I haven't read it yet, silly.' Chloe said with no trace of guilt in her voice.

'I guess you didn't need to.' Megan tried again.

Chloe laughed.

'I'm not psychic! Although Cath did say I had a spooky way of understanding the guests.' She turned to Megan then with a look of wonder on her face. 'Do you think I *could* be psychic?' Her voice was full of such optimism at the thought that Megan had to admit her amateur detective skills were screaming: 'It isn't her!'

Megan sat herself down in a free chair with a sigh.

'I've no idea, Chloe. Not really my area of expertise.'

Chloe shrugged, but continued to

stare out the window.

'I do need to talk to you, actually. You see, the local paper has run another story about us, about the cattery, and it doesn't really show us in a good light; and so I was wondering if you had, you know, accidentally talked to a reporter.'

Chloe's attention wandered from the window to Megan's face, and again she looked confused. 'What would a reporter look like?'

'Probably someone you've never met before.' Megan tried to keep all signs of annoyance from her voice, knowing it wouldn't help.

'Then it wasn't me,' said Chloe. 'Everyone I spoke to yesterday, I've known for years.'

'Do any of them work for a newspaper?' Megan asked slowly. Chloe thought about it for a moment.

'Rascal's mum, Mrs Partridge, she delivers the Parish Newsletter. Does that count?'

Megan smiled; she did feel a little relieved. It seemed unlikely Chloe was the leak.

'No, I think she's safe.' Megan said. 'It must be Graham, then,' she added with a frown, not looking forward to another awkward conversation.

Chloe chuckled. 'Don't be daft! Graham's not been speaking to anyone. Hardly said two words to me, and I've known him since I was small.'

Now it was Megan's turn to stare out of the window. She knew that Chloe was right. Graham might not like her much, as the new owner, but he barely spoke at all, so it seemed unlikely he had sold his story to a local news reporter. Her heart sank as she reached the only plausible explanation. It was Greg. Greg who had seemed too lovely, so understanding and funny. He had asked her about the incident, after all, and she had told him everything; and then he had gone and sold his story to the local paper. Megan couldn't work out what hurt more. The fact that he had probably made a few quid from selling her story, or the fact that she had been taken in by his nice-guy routine.

When Megan's phone beeped for the fourth time, she promised herself she would simply ignore it. She had had several texts from Greg already. The first one all jolly — *How are you?* The second was *Everything okay?* and the last, *Is something wrong?* Definitely the sign of a guilty conscience, Megan decided. She had briefly thought that perhaps it was evidence that he really liked her. That was a thought which made her feel warm and fuzzy on the inside, but then she forced herself to remember how she'd felt when she'd read the front page of the newspaper that morning. That memory extinguished the warm feeling and replaced it with growing embarrassment. She couldn't believe that she had been so taken in, just like a teenage girl who had finally been noticed by the cool boy. So she had decided to ignore him and his texts. Hopefully her silence would give out the message that she had seen through his deception.

The shrill ringtone of her phone

made her jump. Without looking, she knew who it was, and she forced herself to continue to stir the pan of beans that she had warming on the stove for her dinner. Surely ignoring texts and then a phone call would get her message across.

Her phone beeped to tell her that she had a new voicemail. Whilst Megan was pleased that she was standing firm, she couldn't help but feel a little disappointed. She had liked Greg, and so not only was she saddened that he wasn't who he had appeared to be, she was also feeling a little lost at losing her first new friend. A new friend who she had dared to hope might turn into something more . . . She sighed as she turned off the stove and poured her beans over the waiting toast.

Sat at the small kitchen table, she picked up her fork and was just about to eat the first mouthful when the doorbell rang. Megan rolled her eyes at Old Man, who was at his usual sentry post on the windowsill, and whose expression mirrored her own. 'Who's that?' she grumbled, not in the mood to entertain guests. She was considering whether to ignore it or not, hoping perhaps that they would give up and go away, when the doorbell rang again. Whoever it was, wasn't going to go away until she answered.

Using the edge of the kitchen table she hauled herself upright, wincing at the growling pain in her toes, and limped down the hall to the front door. By the time she had made her way there, the doorbell had been rung yet again, and she was thoroughly fed up. She yanked open the front door, not even trying to hide the gathering storm of irritation on her face, but managing to bite back the 'What?' that was on her lips.

Standing on the doorstep was Greg, dressed in a sharp charcoal-grey business suit and clutching a designer black leather laptop bag.

11

Megan stood still and stared. She couldn't quite believe the man had the nerve to actually turn up at her house. Who did he think he was? And, possibly more importantly, how stupid did he think *she* was?

'Are you okay?' he asked, and Megan thought he looked genuinely worried, but firmly reminded herself that she had been fooled before. She could feel him searching her face, and also saw his expression change from one of concern to a frown. Finally, his eyes settled on the surgical boot and her one-legged stance, and widened.

'What on earth happened? I think you should be sitting down.'

'I was, until the doorbell rang,' Megan answered stonily.

'I'm sorry, I had no idea. When you didn't answer my texts I was getting worried, and now I know I had reason to.'

Megan felt her certainty that she knew what was going on falter a little. Why was he being so nice? Maybe he was going to leak another story about her being incompetent, and now injured? She wasn't about to let that happen. The longer she was upright, the more her foot throbbed, so she knew that she needed to tell him to go — and quickly.

'Look, Greg,' she said, 'let's not beat around the bush. I know it was you, and that pretty much puts an end to everything else. As you have pointed out, my foot hurts when I stand up, so I'm going to close the door now and go to sit down.'

One thing Megan was now certain of was that Greg was a great actor. He looked totally bemused and a little hurt.

'You should definitely sit down, but I've no idea what you are talking about.' He gestured for her to move into the house, and with a sigh she swivelled round on one foot. She had been hoping to avoid an extended scene, but clearly one was going to happen regardless. He was going to deny it, and they would go back and forth for a while until Megan saw an opportunity to tell him to leave. She headed back to the kitchen, figuring she should at least eat her supper; also, the kitchen chairs weren't that comfortable, and so hopefully he would get the hint.

When Megan was finally settled back into her chair at the table, she looked up at Greg, who again was displaying all the appropriate signs of sympathy.

'Let me make you a drink,' he offered. 'Tea? Coffee? Or something stronger?'

'Tea, if you're making. I'm taking painkillers so can't drink.' She knew she ought to offer him a beer or some wine but she didn't want to prolong the agony any longer than she needed too.

Greg busied himself making tea. 'So, what on earth happened? I knew something was wrong.'

Megan stared at his back, wondering

how best to start this. With the tiredness, the disappointment, and the pain, she was in no mood for small talk.

'If I tell you, can I expect it to be the headline in the local paper tomorrow?'

Greg chuckled, and Megan frowned: that was not the reaction she had been expecting. Did he think it was funny, letting the local reporter drag her name and the name of Auntie Cath's beloved business through the mud?

'So am I to take it that this is one of those embarrassing stories that we all have?' He turned and place a steaming mug of tea in front of her, then seemed to take a step back when he saw her thunderous expression. Warily, he took a seat opposite her.

'Okay, so I'm clearly missing something here.' He paused for a moment as if he were racking his brains for the answer. 'Did you hurt your foot when we were out last night? Did *I* hurt your foot?' He looked both concerned and confused. 'You didn't say anything,' he added as an afterthought as Megan watched him replay the events of their evening out in his head.

Megan was not going to play this game.

'This isn't about my foot, which I hurt after I got home last night. This is about the front page of the local paper today.'

Greg's look of innocence was pretty convincing. 'I haven't see it today. Came straight here from the airport. What garbage have they gone for now?'

Megan could feel him studying her closely, and so she tried to keep her face neutral before nodding her head in the direction she had tossed the paper, now lying on the kitchen counter. Silently, Greg stood and picked it up, turning it over so he could read the headline. He shook his head.

'They wouldn't know a newsworthy story if they fell over it,' he said, looking up. Megan raised one cool eyebrow, an expression she had mastered after years of dealing with less-than-forthcoming ward staff. She found it best in these situations to say nothing: guilty people always felt the need to fill the silence.

'I can understand that you're put out, but I think most people will laugh it off as ridiculous.'

Megan gritted her teeth.

'The story *is* ridiculous. Of course I'm not happy about it, but what really concerns me is how they got hold of it.'

Greg looked thoughtful, but didn't say anything, and Megan could feel herself getting more exasperated.

'So what I'm saying,' she said, practically hissing the words out, 'is that only three people knew about what happened: Chloe, Graham and you.' She placed as much emphasis on the word *you* as possible, desperate for this conversation to be over so that she could fall into bed and pull the covers over her head and wait for it to be the next day.

'Graham seems unlikely. He hasn't said more than two words to me,' Greg mused, seemingly missing all of Megan's connotations. 'Chloe, then?' But even as he said it he frowned. 'I guess she might have told someone by mistake? You know, not realising what she was doing?'

Megan shook her head. 'It wasn't Chloe; I've already had it out with her.'

Greg's face suddenly looked as if a lightbulb had been turned on behind his eyes. Megan couldn't work out if he was being deliberately slow, or if he couldn't believe that she thought he was the leak.

'You don't think it was me?' he said incredulously. 'I would never do that.' And now he looked indignant, and Megan had a hollow feeling in the pit of her stomach that somehow — she didn't know how — she might have got this horribly wrong. Later, she would wonder if it was that expression that had saved their friendship, as Greg took one look at her before sliding into the chair beside her.

'Megan,' he said, 'I know we've only just met, but I would never do that, never betray your trust. Why would I?' he added, clearly thinking that logic was the way forward. 'I like you, and I think you like me, so why would I risk that?'

Megan could feel herself blush. She hadn't really thought this through, being so blinded with embarrassment and anger.

'I thought you might have done it for the money,' she mumbled, and jumped when Greg laughed warmly.

'I've no idea how much the local rag pays for a headline story, but I don't expect it would cover a round of beer at the pub.' He smiled at her, and Megan felt like maybe she had ruined everything with her assumption.

'I'm a successful businessman, Megan. I don't need to supplement my income by betraying new friends to the local reporter.'

Megan looked down at her plate, feeling even more embarrassed than she had when she had read the headlines.

'But then who?' she wondered out loud.

Greg reached out tentatively for her hand, and she didn't pull away.

'Well, the pub was packed, and we weren't exactly whispering. Anyone could have overheard,' he said with a shrug. 'Although I can't imagine anyone would have a grudge against you . . . ' His voice trailed off, and Megan knew they had both reached the same conclusion.

The only person that Megan had had a run-in with, the only person who had been unfriendly and vocal about her ability to run Cath's Cats, had been at the pub. Doctor William Wakefield, local vet, haughty and judgmental.

'He wouldn't have done it for the money, of course,' Greg said, looking her in the eye, 'but I wouldn't put it past him to do it out of spite.'

12

'Megan! Come quick!' The yell was so urgent and insistent that Megan fell into a sort of hopping run from the office and down the long corridor that contained all the cat pens.

'What is it?' she asked with no little effort, breathless with pain.

'It's Sophia! What are we going to do?' Chloe was wringing her hands and staring into the last luxury cat apartment.

Megan followed Chloe's gaze. Sophia was the ultimate princess cat. She was a purebred Persian with stunning long blue-grey fur that required hours of daily brushing to keep it shining. She wore a diamond-encrusted pink collar that was worth more than Megan's car. Right now, Sophie was crouched on one of the cat shelves near the ceiling of her apartment, and she did not look happy. Her eyes were angry slits, and she hissed and wriggled, but didn't appear to move.

'She's stuck!' Chloe wailed so loudly that the surrounding cats joined in with their own yowls.

'What do you mean, she's stuck? How can she be stuck?' Megan took a tentative step into the enclosure and Sophia hissed viciously.

Chloe turned to Megan with wide eyes. 'I think she must have glued herself there in some kind of protest at the food.'

Megan took a deep breath.

'Don't be ridiculous, Chloe. Where would she have got glue from?' Megan rolled her eyes at herself. Now she was getting pulled into ridiculous thoughts and conversations. 'There must be a logical explanation. Where's Graham?'

'He's painting the back of the apartments. But I don't think he will help. He doesn't like cats much.'

Megan's shoulders sagged. She wasn't surprised that Graham didn't like cats. As far as she could tell, Graham didn't like anything. It was, however, apparent that he didn't give much thoughts to their guests when he went about his maintenance tasks.

'Has he painted the back of Sophia's cage?' she asked, pinching the bridge of her nose to ward off the inevitable headache that she could feel building.

'That's where he started this morning. He did the sides too.'

'And you didn't think to suggest that painting whilst we had a guest in there might not be a good idea?'

Chloe's blank face told her that she wasn't following.

'Chloe, some of the paint has obviously dripped onto the shelf where Sophia is sat, and now it's dried.'

Once again, realisation dawned on Chloe like the sun rising. 'Oh, poor Sophia. What are we going to do?'

Megan peered a little closer, despite Sophia's warning growl.

'I think if you can hold her, I can snip off the fur that's stuck. So we should be able to do it without hurting her.'

Chloe looked doubtful, and Megan could feel her own anxiety at the state Sophia was in mix with anger, Chloe was supposed to be the cat whisperer.

'I don't think Sophia will let me get near her,' Chloe said reaching out a heavily gauntleted hand, which Sophia immediately bit into with her sharp teeth. Her wince, when she had never before been fazed by misbehaviour of the guests in the form of scratches and nips, told Megan that she was right. 'I think we've going to need the vet to give her something to chill out.'

Megan knew that Chloe was right, but it still made her heart sink.

'I'll go and see if I can find a vet on the internet,' Megan said, determined that Doctor Wakefield wasn't going to get any more of her business — or what was left of her business after all this.

Chloe sucked in air. 'Sophia only goes to see Doctor Wakefield. Mr George-town won't have her seen by anyone else.'

Megan's shoulders sagged. Of course,

that *would* be the case, wouldn't it? Gloomily, she stomped off in the direction of the telephone to make the dreaded call, all the while wondering if she could get her old job back, since her new career wasn't working out so well.

After phoning, Megan sent Chloe around to the front of the bungalow to wait for Doctor Wakefield, thinking that she wanted to delay seeing him for as long as possible. She wasn't sure how she would react to his aloof judgement of yet another feline fail on her part, especially since she now knew that he was trying to undermine her cattery by sharing what he heard in the pub with a local reporter. She wondered if he was hoping to take it over himself, to grow his own business. She raised her eyebrow at the thought as she tried to make cooing noises at Sophia, who was getting angrier at her statue state by the second.

When she'd gone to bed the night before, she had imagined a whole range of scenarios where she challenged him over his behaviour — some in public where others could see his shame — but she knew that this was not the time to confront him. Right now, they needed to get Sophia sorted, and then Megan would have to work out how she was going to explain this to Mr Georgetown.

Doctor Wakefield stalked down the path, needing no words to express what he was obviously thinking. Disdain seemed to wash off him, and he greeted Megan with a mere nod before he turned his attention to his patient.

'Sophia,' he said in a surprisingly soft tone. 'What have you got yourself into this time?'

Megan blinked in surprise. Gone was the 'small animals are beneath me' attitude, and in its place was that of a Doctor Doolittle wannabe. Whatever was going on, it appeared to be working; after one final, rather half-hearted hiss, to Megan's astonishment there was the rumble of a soft purr. Glancing at Chloe, who was looking awestruck — either that, or thinking really hard — Megan realised that whatever else Doctor Wakefield was, he was a miracle worker when it came to animals.

'Chloe,' Doctor Wakefield said in the same soft tone, 'could you look in my bag and see if you can find my scissors?'

Chloe just stood and stared, clearly too under his spell to move. Despite everything, Megan had to agree that, on this occasion, he seemed to be weaving some kind of enchantment.

Megan unclasped his case and found all inside neat and orderly. She quickly located a pair of slightly curved scissors, and stepped in to the pen as quietly as she could with her surgical booted foot. Apart from a quick glance down and a frown, Doctor Wakefield continued to stroke the now-compliant Sophia, and talked to her softly.

'I think perhaps,' he said without turning to Megan, 'it might be a good idea for you to see if you can trim Sophia's fur. I would like to avoid a sedative if at all possible.'

Megan gently lifted Sophia's tail so that she could see better, and the cat wriggled indignantly. She paused, and allowed Doctor Wakefield to do his calming thing. Once Sophia was still again, Megan felt for the bone and flesh of her tail and carefully started to trim the fur, as near as to the painted surface as possible. With practiced, steady hands, she made her way deftly along the line of tail stuck to the shelf, and within a minute the cat was free.

Sophia, for her part, arched her back, did a stretch that would have made a yoga teacher jealous, and then proceeded to bump her head against Doctor Wakefield's hand as he gently checked her for any signs of injury.

'If I didn't know better, I would have said you'd done that before.'

Megan nearly jumped out of her skin when she realised he was addressing her. In their limited conversations so far, he had never said anything that could be construed as a compliment.

'Animal patients aren't so different from human patients when they are in distress,' she said, feeling completely wrong-footed and not knowing what else to say. To challenge him now about his behaviour seemed beyond churlish, especially since he seemed to be making an effort to be friendly — but then again, Megan thought, perhaps he was just feeling guilty?

'Well, you have the knack,' he said, holding out a treat in his hand for Sophia to nibble on.

'Is she okay?' Megan asked anxiously. Seeing animals in pain or distress was as bad, if not worse, than seeing people in that state; at least with people, she knew what to do to make them feel better.

'No harm done from her little adventure; and trust me, she's had worse.' Doctor Wakefield looked at her for the first time since she arrived, and she thought she saw the glimmer of a smile; certainly his brown eyes seemed to be giving that message.

113

'I don't think Mr Georgetown is going to be too impressed,' she said ruefully, before realising she had spoken the words out loud. She would have kicked herself, but that didn't seem to be such a good idea since she already had one injured foot.

'Don't worry about old Jeffery. Sophia gets into more scrapes at home. He's used to it. I can talk to him if you're concerned.'

Doctor Wakefield had turned his attention back to tickling Sophia behind her ears, and so Megan couldn't clearly see his expression. She really couldn't work out what was going on — it was as if he had had a personality transplant. Could it really be guilt? Megan wasn't sure, and despite the fact that she could feel herself thawing towards him, she still had her doubts.

'Thanks for the offer, but I'm sure I can sort things out with Mr Georgetown. Now, what do I owe you?'

Doctor Wakefield didn't seem bothered by her last statement, so Megan took that as a good sign that she hadn't insulted him or done anything to provoke a deterioration in their new civil communication style. He picked up his case and walked out of the pen.

'No charge. I was about to go out on my rounds, so it was on my way.'

Megan stopped and stared, before remembering to close the door behind her. She didn't need a lost cat to add to her woes.

'I really think I should pay. I've taken up some of your time at the very least.'

He walked up the path to the door that led out to the garden, waving a hand as if to say it was nothing. Megan stood where she was and watched him go. What she needed now was a cup of coffee and to rest her foot; then she would try and make sense of everything that had just happened with the confusingly mysterious Doctor Wakefield.

13

After a cup of coffee and more chocolate biscuits than she should have eaten, Megan still could not figure out what on earth had just happened. Haughty, unpleasant Doctor Wakefield had somehow morphed into gentle, almost friendly Doctor Wakefield. She had wondered if guilt were a factor, but that just didn't seem to fit with the man she had met on her first visit to the vet. She doubted that he would ever feel guilty about anything. He, presumably, would feel that he was doing the right thing, and he had the right to do it. No, she just couldn't make that idea fit with what had just happened.

'Maybe I was wrong about him,' she said to Belle, who had deftly jumped into her lap looking for some attention. 'I probably shouldn't give up my day job to become a private eye, either.' She scratched Belle behind the ears. 'So far, it seems I have followed the clues and accused two innocent people who have actually turned out to be quite nice.'

Megan leaned back in her chair. But if it wasn't Greg and it wasn't Doctor Wakefield, then who was it? The realisation that she would just to wait and see what tomorrow's papers brought filled her with gloom, and so she reached for another chocolate biscuit.

When the doorbell rang that evening, Megan was pleased. She had purposefully left it on the latch so she wouldn't have to move from her position on the sofa with her poorly foot propped up on pillows, and she knew who it was. Greg had texted her to ask if she wanted some company — and, even better news, he was going to bring a takeaway with him.

'It's only Greg,' he called from the hallway.

'In here,' Megan called back.

Greg appeared through the lounge door, and the delicious smell of Chinese takeaway filled the room. Megan's tummy rumbled in appreciation. Greg laughed.

'Sounds like I've come at the right time. I'll just grab some plates and bits from the kitchen.' He dished up the food and handed Megan a plate.

'So, I hear on the grapevine that you had a visit from our friendly local vet. Did he pop round to gloat, or was he simply here to point out what you were doing wrong?' Greg grinned and Megan frowned a little.

'Actually, I had to call him,' she replied, thinking back to what Greg had said about Doctor Wakefield and her own experience.

'Oh, everything alright?' he asked, his expression changing to concern.

'Everything's fine now, but no thanks to Graham.'

Greg raised a questioning eyebrow as he took a mouthful of food. Megan sighed at the memory of the conversation she had had with Sophia's owner — who, thankfully, had been very understanding, and even apologised for the trouble that Sophia had caused.

'Graham decided to paint the sheds, and some of the paint dripped on to one of the shelves inside the pen.'

'Okay . . . ' Greg said, clearly not seeing the connection between fresh paint and the need to call a vet. 'You know, if you needed someone to consult with on paint colours, I would probably be the better bet.'

Megan rolled her eyes at him. 'One of the residents decided to sit on the wet shelf.'

'Ah, so you had a cat covered in paint. I bet that was fun to get off.'

'Actually, it was worse than that. We had a cat *stuck* to the shelf. She'd sat down when the paint was wet, and it dried. Hey presto — one stuck cat.'

Greg coughed as he tried to swallow a mouthful of food and laugh at the same time. Megan waited as he composed himself.

'I'm sorry. That is obviously not funny,' he said, in a way that suggested he was telling himself off before she had the chance to.

Megan shrugged. 'Well, it wasn't that funny at the time; but since Sophia is none the worse for wear and her owner isn't threatening to sue, I think I can now see the funny side. I just can't work out why all this stuff keeps happening to me.'

'You do seem to have a gift for it.'

'More like a gift for the local reporter,' Megan said, suddenly feeling like the gloomy mood was returning at the thought of the local newspaper appearing on her doormat the following morning.

'You think Wakefield will talk to the press again? Might be a bit obvious, even for him.'

Megan looked up at the ceiling, lost in thought.

'Greg to Megan, come in Megan,' he joked, and she looked at him with a smile.

'I'm not so sure it is him,' she said. 'He was like a completely different person today, and you should have seen how he handled Sophia.'

Greg snorted. 'I would expect him to

be good at that after all that expensive training.'

Megan watched Greg as he continued to eat, and started to wonder if there was more to his opinion of Doctor Wakefield than he let on.

'What is it between you and him? I'm getting the definite vibe that there is more to it than what you've told me.'

Megan watched as Greg's expression darkened, and she knew that she had hit the nail on the head.

'It's in the past, but something that's hard to forget,' Greg said, staring moodily into the beer in his glass.

'I'm sorry,' Megan said. 'I don't mean to pry.'

Greg shook his head. 'You aren't, and it's not exactly a secret. I develop property. I have a real passion for saving old property and restoring it to its former glory.'

Megan nodded to show she understood, but said nothing, not wanting to interrupt his flow.

'Well, the site where the vet clinic is

now was once this beautiful set of farm labourer's cottages. Not special enough to be listed or anything, but an important part of the village's heritage. I had a bid in to buy them and a provisional agreement with the owners, and then flashy Doctor Wakefield arrives, offering so much money that the elderly couple simply couldn't refuse. I don't blame them: the old guy was in a wheelchair due to arthritis, and they needed all the money they could get for his care. And so Doctor Wakefield got what he wanted, and destroyed part of the village's history as he did it. Cost me a fair bit of money, too. Not really important in the grand scheme of things, but I feel like I spend my life fighting against people like him. People from outside who arrive and want to change everything.' As he uttered the last words, the colour started to rise in his cheeks. 'I don't mean you, of course,' he added hurriedly.

Megan smiled. 'I know exactly what you mean.'

They sat in silence for a few

moments, both lost in thought.

'It did occur to me that perhaps that might be the motivation for trying to discredit me, to try and get me to sell up or something.' Megan shrugged, as it still didn't quite add up.

'I hadn't thought of it that way,' Greg said. 'But you could be right. I certainly wouldn't put it past him after my experiences. I know his business is doing well, so maybe he's looking to expand.'

Megan wriggled uncomfortably. It made sense, but something was not sitting right, and she couldn't work out what it was.

'Perhaps we should talk about something else. We've wasted enough of our evening discussing the awful Wakefield character. Tell me about your life in London.'

And with that, the conversation moved on, much to Megan's relief.

14

Megan had a restless night, despite the fact that she had left the bedroom door open so the cats could come and go as they pleased. Both Belle and Tinker had curled up on the end of the bed, and Megan suspected that they would have slept through the night, had her tossing and turning not repeatedly disturbed them. In the early hours, they appeared to be quite disgruntled, and they both sashayed from the room with tails in the air and imaginary eyebrows raised.

Megan lay in bed unable to sleep, or even doze, and she knew that there would be no more rest. She was waiting for the tell-tale soft thud that would tell her the local newspaper had been delivered and was now lying on the doormat. As she lay on her back staring at the ceiling, her mind raced. She still could not figure out who had it in for her, and why. The idea that anyone was selling these stories to make a quick buck seemed laughable, since the local newspaper couldn't possibly pay much money in light of their small readership. That left other motives that made Megan wriggle uncomfortably at the thought that it was something more personal than that.

Her mind drifted back to the conversation with Greg last night. His story about Doctor Wakefield would certainly fit with her first meeting with the vet at the clinic, and his reaction in the pub, but not at all with their last encounter. Though maybe that was just guilt? Guilt at having to deal with that person face to face, and realising that the business you were trying to ruin had a very real person behind it?

Megan sighed, rolled over, and got out of bed. A detective, she wasn't. She'd always thought she was a good judge of character, but clearly she had left that skill back in London. What she needed now was a cup of strong coffee before she faced what the newspaper would bring.

Megan had managed to limp to the threshold of the kitchen when the warning thud told her the newspaper had now arrived and was ready to be read. She stiffened, but decided to stick to her original plan, so it was with freshly made coffee in one hand that she lifted the paper from the mat — and instantly regretted it.

ANOTHER CAT-ASTROPHE AT
CATH'S CATS!

We are sorry to report that another feline has fallen foul of a catastrophe at Cath's Cats. Sophia Georgetown, the beautiful and much-loved pedigree Persian cat of local resident Jeffery Georgetown, has experienced a most traumatic event at the hands of the new — and who can only be described as inexperienced — owner of the cattery. For some reason known only to Megan Fullstaff, the decision was taken to paint the inside of the pens whilst a cat was in residence. This foolhardy, even downright hazardous, decision resulted in Mr Georgetown's precious pet become stuck fast to dried paint and requiring the attention of local vet Doctor William Wakefield.

Doctor Wakefield was required to remove a significant portion of poor Sophia's luxurious fur in order to release her from her predicament, and we understand that Sophia is now being treated for a nervous condition which was brought on by the shock of the terrible experience. Mr Jeffery Georgetown, Sophia's devoted owner, was too upset to comment about the awful treatment his beloved pet had experienced at the hands of the new cattery manager, but we are led to believe that Sophia will not be taking her usual place at the famous Little River Cat Show in three weeks' time.

Megan snorted at the last comment. Clearly they had tried to get Mr Georgetown to make an on-the-record comment, and when he had refused — or perhaps said something they didn't want to hear — they had made up that ridiculous story. When Megan had spoken to him, once she had reassured him that Sophia was none the worse for her experience, he had simply laughed and told her that Sophia got into much more hair-raising scrapes at home, and she shouldn't worry about it. Her expression darkened as she considered where the information had come from. Would Doctor Wakefield have said he was treating Sophia for a nervous condition? That was blatantly not true, but it would be difficult for her to argue if the paper had him on record. He was, after all, the well-respected local vet, and she was the hopelessly incompetent — if not down-right neglectful — new owner of the local cattery.

One thing was certain: she could

expect more cancellations today. Something they definitely didn't need. The thought of it made her angry. If Doctor Wakefield or anyone else was expecting her to just take this lying down, then they were very much mistaken. All it did was make her more determined. There was no way she was going to let someone bully her out of running Auntie Cath's cattery as it had always been — a small but successful business. That had been Auntie Cath's legacy and her final wish, and there was no way that Megan was going to let her down. Auntie Cath had obviously believed she was going to be able to do it, and so whatever happened, she would.

Megan was sat in the small office with her foot on a box of cat food when the doorbell to the cattery rang. She took one look at the diary which held the bookings, and frowned: no one was due to pick up or drop off and so that meant only one thing. Another customer, the third that morning who had come to pick up their feline early. She fixed her expression to one of professional unconcern.

Although her toes were slowly improving, she had left the surgical boot on, and so she still hobbled rather than walked. She was nearly at the gate when the bell rang again, and she had to quash down the sense of impatience that she felt, knowing it would not help the situation. She took a deep breath before opening the gate, and made sure her face displayed none of the feelings she felt on the inside — that was, until she realised who the person on the other side was. She was not mentally prepared to see, let alone speak to, Doctor William Wakefield.

'Morning, Miss Falstaff. I thought I would pop in and check on Sophia.'

He was dressed in a crisp mid-blue polo shirt which was embroidered with his name and qualifications, as well as the name of his practice. He wore navy-blue combat trousers. It all screamed 'money' to Megan, and he would not have looked out of place at the Henley Royal Regatta. He carried his black leather case, and his handsome features betrayed nothing.

'Miss Falstaff?' he asked again, this time a little impatiently. Clearly he was not a man used to be left waiting.

'Sorry,' Megan said automatically, even though she knew she shouldn't be apologising to the man who quite possibly was trying to ruin her business — Auntie Cath's business. 'I wasn't expecting you to visit today.'

She moved a step to the side to allow him to walk past her, and watched him stride down the path. Despite his words, there seemed no explanation, no reason, for him being there. Was this more evidence that he was behind it all?

15

Doctor Wakefield nodded his head at Chloe, who looked like a teenager meeting her pop hero. Megan almost expected her to curtsey. She wondered if Chloe would view him in quite the same light if she knew what Megan suspected he had been doing behind their backs.

'How is Sophia today?' he asked Chloe, who took a moment to shake herself from her admiration to answer.

'She seems fine — well, a little put out. I mean, you would be too if you'd had to be cut off a newly painted shelf, wouldn't you?'

Megan winced at Chloe's interpretations of the previous day's events.

'She is a cat who is very proud of her appearance,' Chloe continued blithely, 'and I think personally that she thought her tail was her best asset; and now it looks like she's going through a punk rocker phase.'

Doctor Wakefield turned then, and Megan braced herself, expecting some sort of haughty lecture; but, to her surprise, he was smiling warmly. Megan had no choice but to join Chloe in her admiration. When he smiled, it transformed him. His eyes seemed to light up, and his face showed a vulnerability that was not normally there.

'Well, as Mr Georgetown would say, she's definitely a looker and she knows it. The fur will grow back in a month or so, and she will be back to her preening glory.'

Megan blinked, not able to work out which of these several personalities was the real Doctor Wakefield. He seemed so human in that moment, not the haughty caricature that he wore like a mask most of the time. Or was this, the human and attractive side of him, the caricature? Was this all for her benefit? To lull her into thinking he couldn't possibly be the whistle-blower?

Megan leaned against a post, taking some of the weight off her foot, and watched as Sophia responded to Doctor Wakefield in much the same way that Chloe had. Gone was the crotchety, aloof feline; now here was one that was literally rolling on her back with her legs in the air so that her tummy could be tickled.

'She seems none the worse for wear for her adventure,' he said as he stepped back out of the pen, Sophia trotting at his heels.

Megan crossed her arms. She was fed up with the amateur detective routine. She needed to know, she had to find out, who was behind all this, or she would go mad.

'That's not what the paper said this morning.' She raised one eyebrow in what she hoped would be received as a pointed message. She watched closely for his reaction. Something crossed his face, a fleeting emotion, but it was too quick for Megan to interpret.

'The papers?' he said — whether

acting or actually confused, she wasn't sure.

'Perhaps you didn't need to read them, since you knew what would be in them.' The words spilled out, and inwardly Megan cursed herself for letting her emotions take over her brain. Chloe was staring between the two of them as if she were watching a tennis match.

'Why would I know what was in the paper?' Doctor Wakefield replied coldly, as if such a thing were completely beneath him.

'Well, someone has been talking to them, and they seemed to know a lot about your visit yesterday,' Megan said. Despite her best efforts, his transformation back to Haughty Doctor Wakefield was prodding at her temper.

'And so you naturally assumed it was me.' His voice had gone from cold to glacial, and he looked furious at even the suggestion he would do something so ungentlemanly.

'I'm not sure . . . ' Megan said,

feeling herself quake a little at his disapproval. ' . . . but I wanted to ask, to clear the air,' she added feebly.

'I wasn't aware that the air needed clearing, Miss Falstaff.' She watched as he turned and picked up his case. 'Sophia is recovering and won't require further visits, so I would anticipate that our paths won't cross again.'

And with that he was striding back through the cattery pens and out of the gate that led to the drive, Megan and Chloe staring after him.

'I think he fancies you,' Chloe said with awe in her voice.

Megan laughed bitterly. 'I think the opposite is true.'

'What was that all about?'

'Have you seen the paper this morning?' Megan asked.

Chloe nodded. 'Where did they get that story from?' she asked, her expression quite serious — possibly the first time Megan had ever seen her look like that.

'That's the point,' Megan said

looking in the direction in which Doctor Wakefield had just left. Chloe seemed to consider that for a few moments, and then her eyes went wide. 'You think it was him?'

Megan shrugged; she still didn't know, not really.

'He was here, I suppose,' Chloe said, and then screwed up her face. 'But he wouldn't. He's not that sort of bloke.'

'If it wasn't him,' Megan said ominously, 'then who was it?'

And to that, Chloe didn't have any answer.

*   *   *

Megan was finding it hard to concentrate on anything else. The question seemed ever-present in her mind, no matter how hard she tried to concentrate, or focus on whatever she needed to do to keep the business going. Auntie Cath had never really needed to advertise, but Megan was fairly sure she hadn't had bad press, either. Megan had been looking at options to advertise to a wider audience, and thinking about whether she could afford to get a website up and running. From the few books she had bought about running one's own business, this seemed to be the way forward. Being IT-phobic, the only way this was going to happen was if she could scrape together the money to pay for it.

She had looked online at other catteries before finding herself plugging 'Doctor William Wakefield' into the search engine. She did a quick check outside — Chloe was down at the far end of the pens, and Graham was rustling around in the shed where his tools lived, and where he hid at every opportunity. The computer beeped, and her screen was filled with a list of references to Doctor William Wakefield. The first one appeared to be the website for the clinic. She clicked on it, and it was as flash as she had imagined. A professional photograph of Doctor Wakefield, standing with his arms crossed across his broad chest and a solemn expression, stared at her, and she felt like it was judging her somehow. She wondered if he would be able to tell that she had been looking at his website, and the mere thought of that made her click out, feeling guilty.

'You look like you are up to something you shouldn't be,' a voice said just behind her, and Megan jumped so badly that her knees knocked painfully on the underside of the small desk. She gave herself a minute to push down the hurt, and swivelled round in the chair.

'Sorry, didn't mean to make you jump,' Greg said, dressed in a smart business suit and clutching two takeaway cups. The smell of the freshly brewed coffee made her smile.

'I come bearing gifts,' Greg said, handing over a drink.

'Thanks. It's like you can read my mind.'

'In that case, I also hope you are in the mood for a pastry. Fresh from the bakery?' He looked hopeful, like he really wanted to please her; and so, despite the fact that she had eaten more chocolate biscuits the day before than was good for her, she gratefully accepted before gesturing him to the spare chair.

'Other than bringing much-needed supplies, what brings you here?'

His face told her everything she needed to know.

'Ah,' she said, taking a bite from her chocolate plait, which melted softly in her mouth. 'I take it you have read the paper.'

He grimaced and took a sip of his coffee.

'Didn't get round to it till lunchtime, or I would have come sooner.'

'You didn't have to, you know.' Megan blew out a sigh. 'I'm almost getting used to it. You know, wake up in the morning, and find that you are the subject of local gossip which is only half-true.' She shrugged as if she didn't quite know how to finish.

'I'm really sorry, Megan. I want you to know that everyone I speak to, I tell them it's not true.'

He looked so earnest then that Megan couldn't help but giggle. 'You make it sound like you are out defending my honour.'

'I sort of feel I am,' he said, sounding a bit sheepish. Megan felt a pang of guilt and reached out a hand for his arm.

'Sorry, I didn't mean to sound ungrateful. I am thankful, really. It's good to know that I have at least one friend and ally here.'

She waited until he met her gaze, and then she smiled at him. He looked thoughtful, and Megan felt like there was more going on behind his eyes than she was aware of. Then he leaned over and kissed her softly on the lips.

16

His touch was gentle, and Megan felt herself relax into the kiss. A small part of her mind thought that Auntie Cath was probably looking down and smiling, having been convinced and vocal about the fact that she thought it was time for Megan to settle down and find a good man. She felt his hand brush a hair away from her face, and then Greg pulled back.

'Sorry,' he murmured, although he was smiling a little, 'couldn't resist the urge to kiss you.'

Megan tilted her head to one side and moved so that she could kiss him back, as if in answer to his question. She found herself gently tugged from her chair into his lap, his arms holding her tight. Sunlight seemed to fill the room, and Megan knew that this was what had been missing from her life for too long. Romance, love, or closeness to another, she wasn't sure. Except that it felt right.

'Dinner tonight?' Greg asked, slightly breathless when they finally parted. 'We'll go out of the village, somewhere we can get away from everyone? Just you and me?'

'Sounds perfect,' Megan said. Greg studied her closely for a couple of heartbeats, and she felt like he was trying to memorise her face.

'I have to get back to work,' he said, his voice full of reluctance. 'But I'll pick you up at six-thirty.'

And then he was gone, and all Megan could do was lean back in the chair and thank Auntie Cath for being right as usual. Her life at London had become a work-dominated monotony. She hadn't felt so free and happy for a long time. She missed Auntie Cath desperately, though. Despite not being blood family, Cath had been both a mother and an auntie to Megan — but it felt good to think that she was doing what Cath had always wanted her to do, taking over the business and find some measure of personal happiness. She looked back at the computer, knowing that she should turn her attention to finding a web designer who wouldn't completely wipe out her savings, but instead closed the lid and headed inside to pick an outfit suitable for that night.

★　★　★

The evening had gone quickly, as time often seemed to when you were enjoying yourself. Greg had chosen a small French restaurant with a long orangery on one side which, despite the cool evening, meant they had been able to see the stars. It had been one of the most romantic events of Megan's life, and she couldn't help but smile as she pushed her key in to the lock and waved goodbye to Greg, before stepping inside. In the hall she kicked off her flat ballet pumps, the only shoes she could even consider wearing with her still painful toes and sighed with relief. She padded bare foot into the kitchen and it was there that she knew something was terribly wrong.

Old Man wasn't sat in his usual spot on the kitchen windowsill, which in itself was a little odd. There was no sign of Tinker or Belle, either, who would normally greet her with some of the best cat dancing in order to obtain a treat. Megan frowned and turned to the back door. She had never yet had to call the cats in, as they seemed to have a mysterious sense of knowing when she was home. She opened the back door and tried to peer into the darkness.

'Tinker? Belle?' she called into the blackness, and then heard a mournful wail. She grabbed a torch from the kitchen work surface and made her way in the direction of the sound. When she was near to the shed where Graham kept his tools, she could make out two sets of amber eyes, and then the wailing became more urgent.

Megan felt the fear build in her.

Something was wrong. Something had happened to one of Auntie Cath's beloved cats, cats that had become her own little family.

She shown the torch wildly, and it was only when Belle wound around her ankles and she followed her direction that she found him. Old Man was lying on his side, and even in the dim light from the torch, Megan knew something was wrong: he seemed to be panting, his tongue lolling and his eyes half-closed. Megan held back her own wail and lifted him into her arms before hurrying back to the house.

She wrapped Old Man in a warm jumper and laid him carefully on the sofa in the lounge. Tinker and Belle were pacing, and seemed to be trying to give her some feline message that she couldn't interpret. Megan grabbed her phone from her bag, about to ring Greg, and then she knew what she needed to do. Whatever she felt about Doctor Wakefield, at that moment Old Man needed him. He was the only one who could do something for the elderly cat, and Megan's hands shook as she rang the clinic's emergency number.

'Hello?' a voice enquired, slightly sleepy but not asleep. Megan instantly recognised it as Doctor Wakefield's, which surprised her as she had expected some posh answering service to take her call.

'Doctor Wakefield, it's Old Man . . . ' Megan managed to squeeze the words out before her throat closed up with tears.

'Miss Falstaff? I'll be there in ten minutes. Keep him warm if you can.' The voice had gone from sleepy to alert in a heartbeat, and it took Megan a few moments to process that he knew who she was based only on the name of one of Auntie Cath's cats. She slipped to the front door and left it on the latch, then returned to hold vigil beside Tinker and Belle as they waited.

The door was pushed open and Megan could hear footsteps. She tried to find the calm place inside her that she had taught herself to use when she was dealing with a nursing crisis, but she couldn't grab hold of it. The pain of losing Cath was as overwhelming in that moment as it had been on the day of the fateful phone call. To lose Old Man now was not something she thought she could bear. She didn't even try to hold back the tears when Doctor Wakefield walked into the room.

He was wearing jeans and an old t-shirt — clearly he hadn't bothered to waste time getting changed. After looking at Megan with a flash of sympathy, he turned his attention to his patient. He ran his hands over the prone cat, who was now twitching, his eyes rolling. She tried to stifle a moan.

'Was there evidence of vomiting?' His voice was urgent and Megan couldn't find her voice, simply nodded. 'Show me.' He commanded.

They were outside for a matter of moments and then Doctor Wakefield led her back inside, his face set grim.

'It's antifreeze poisoning. I've seen it

before. I'll need to run tests, but we should start treatment as soon as possible. Do you know how long since he developed symptoms?'

'He was fine before I went out. I was gone maybe three hours,' Megan managed to say. Doctor Wakefield nodded.

'That means we've caught it early.' He reached over and placed a hand on her arm, looking her carefully in the eye. 'Old Man is elderly, which is against him, but as we've caught it at this point . . . I can treat him to try and flush his system, so he's in with a chance, but we won't know till morning if it's worked.'

Megan nodded, trying to take it all in; the fact that there was hope made her heart surge just a little.

'Do we need to get him to your place?' she asked, the sensible side of her brain finally starting to kick in. The vet shook his head.

'I can treat him here, if you like. They would probably prefer it,' he said, leaning over and tweaking Belle's ear, who purred in response.

'If you don't mind?' she asked. He shrugged. 'I'll go and make some fresh coffee — it sounds like we're going to need it.'

'That would be lovely,' he said, turning his attention back to Old Man. By the time she had returned, the cat had an intravenous drip in his leg, slowly feeding him fluid, and Wakefield was administrating an injection.

'Bicarbonate,' he said by way of explanation — although whether to Megan or the two cats who sat either side of Old Man like sentries, she wasn't sure.

Megan curled up on the floor by Old Man's head and gently stroked him. Doctor Wakefield sat next to her.

'Is there anything else we can do?' she asked softly.

He shook his head, 'All we can do is watch and wait. It's up to Old Man now.' He accepted the cup of coffee, and they sipped their drinks in silence.

17

They sat there in silence for a while, but it wasn't the awkward kind silence — more of a companionable one.

'Thank you for coming,' Megan said, and she meant it. Whatever else she thought about William Wakefield, he had come through for her and Old Man.

'Of course,' he said with a hint of a smile. 'It's what I do.'

'I'm not sure all vets have that view,' Megan said, remembering what Auntie Cath had said about the previous village vet, who'd kept office hours and not a moment longer.

'It's just like being a nurse, I guess. Your patients don't stop needing you just because the working day for the average person is over.'

Megan nodded; that was certainly true.

'Do you miss it?' he asked suddenly, as if he was worried that he would chicken out if he didn't ask the question straight away.

Megan thought for a moment.

'Yes, I do. I mean, I miss the patients. Being a nurse is a real privilege and I loved the caring side.'

'But?'

Megan smiled at him and their eyes met properly for the first time. She felt drawn into them like she was under a magic spell. She blinked and forced herself to look away. What was she doing? She had been out with a person whom she hoped was her new boyfriend not six hours earlier.

'But,' she said carefully, determined to get back on track, 'there's a lot of politics, a lot of sacrifices.' She shrugged. 'Not dissimilar to your job, I expect.'

He was looking at her curiously, so she forced her attention back to Old Man and gave him a gentle stroke.

'You're right; but since I've become my own boss, I can write my own rulebook. Do things the way I want them done, the way I think they should be done.' He frowned now at his own comment, and Megan pursed her lips to prevent a small laugh escaping. She was too late because he saw it anyway. He ran a hand through his hair, making it stand up at odd angles, it made him look more human, somehow.

'Not that I'm saying I'm always right, of course,' he added rather ruefully. 'It's just I can't stand to see animals mistreated in any way. They do so much for us, the least we can do is care for them in the way they deserve.'

Megan took a few minutes to digest this information. If ever there was a time to get to the bottom of the mystery that was Doctor William Wakefield, it was now.

'So, the day I brought the Colonel in . . .'

Wakefield leaned over and checked Old Man's pulse before nodding in satisfaction.

'I thought that you didn't know what

you were doing. Sometimes my concern comes out a little . . . '

'Haughty and arrogant?' Megan asked innocently, and this time she was rewarded with a laugh.

'Ouch! But okay — I think I deserved that one.'

'You didn't give me much of a chance,' she said, but with a smile.

'You did appear to think that a male cat could have kittens,' he retorted, and then they both laughed — softly, so as not to disturb the three now-sleeping animals.

'Not my finest moment.' Megan agreed. 'In my defence, I'd had a terrible night's sleep, and I thought the Colonel probably needed urgent medical attention.'

'For future reference, cats can pretty much do the birthing thing all by themselves — even cats that have been treated like a boy all their lives have some idea.'

'I know that *now*,' Megan said. 'But in humans that isn't true, and so I'm afraid I defaulted to my best experience of women having babies.' She thought for a few moments. 'More coffee?' she asked, and he nodded his head before checking on Old Man's IV.

Megan returned with a tray and the last of the chocolate biscuits. Doctor Wakefield fell on them as if he hadn't eaten in days.

'There's something about all-nighters that makes me really hungry,' he said. Megan nodded in agreement and then helped herself before they were all gone. She was trying to work out how to ask Doctor Wakefield if it was him who had gone to the papers. What she didn't want to happen was to be stuck with the haughty and upset version of him for another six hours. She doubted he would up and leave — it was clear to her that he took the welfare of his patients very seriously — but it would be a long night if he took umbrage to her question.

'I am curious about one thing,' he said, the late night clearly making him much chattier than before.

'Oh, yes?' Megan asked distractedly as she tried to work out how to casually drop the question she was desperate to ask into the conversation.

'Why did you think that I had gone to the papers?'

Megan blinked, wondering if the man who had such a way with animals was also a mind-reader.

'I . . . er.'

He was looking at her, but she was relieved to see there was no sign of anger — more like slightly hurt curiosity. She swallowed; she had been concentrating so hard on asking a similar question that she had given no thought to how she would answer if he turned the tables on her, as he just had. She looked down and then took a deep breath, reminding herself that she wanted to know, so now she needed to be honest too.

'You didn't seem to like me,' she blurted out and then felt herself blush, grateful that the lighting in the room was low, and hoping he couldn't tell.

'I may have been a little concerned as to whether you were up to looking after the cats in your care.'

She looked up sharply, but he shrugged as if to say, 'First impressions'.

'But it was nothing personal. I guess you could say I had my professional head on me, and unfortunately I've seen it before. Where people are just in it for the money.'

Megan opened her mouth to speak — she felt a little spark of indignation at his words and wanted to correct him, but he held up his hand as if to hold her back.

'It was wrong of me, of course. I knew nothing about you, and I should have known better. Cathleen would not have left this place to you if she didn't trust you implicitly, and she was deeply suspicious of anyone who didn't love animals.'

He looked at her now, and there was almost pleading in his eyes, as if he were begging her to forgive him. She blinked, wondering if her imagination were conjuring up the expression because it was what she wanted to see — but no, it was still there.

'I do love animals, but I guess I have more experience with people. I would never do anything to purposely harm any creature,' she said, and turned her attention back to Old Man, who lay still but was breathing easier. She stroked him gently.

'Caring is the first step, and the rest you can learn,' he said, and now he was smiling.

'I'm not sure there is going to be a business left after all the bad press. I can't help but feel I've let her down,' Megan said, and tried to swallow down the tears that had suddenly appeared. The press had been awful, but the thought of losing Old Man — so soon after Auntie Cath, and to something so horrible as poisoning — was just too awful to contemplate. She sniffed, trying to hold back all the emotions, and a hand reached out to cover hers. That small act of kindness was too much — the delicate wall broke, and the wave of emotion was so fierce that Megan was shaking with the force of it.

'I'm sorry. I didn't mean to upset you.' His voice was soft and tinged with regret.

'You didn't,' Megan managed to say between sobs. She gestured with her free hand to Old Man, and found herself pulled into a hug.

'All the signs are good, Megan. I think Old Man is going to be fine.'

'I can't lose him,' she sobbed. 'Not now, not so soon after Auntie Cath, and not like this.'

'I will do everything I can, and I won't leave him until we know, I promise.'

The tears were flowing so hard now that Megan knew she wouldn't be able to speak. So instead, she returned his hug, and hoped that he would understand how grateful she was to him in that moment.

18

Neither of them slept: too used to keeping the night watch, and too worried to close their eyes in case Old Man should take a turn for the worse. The pale sun started to show its early-morning face, and Megan stretched.

'Breakfast?' she asked quietly.

Doctor Wakefield laughed as Tinker and Belle leapt to their feet and started rubbing themselves against Megan's legs.

'For us or for them?' he asked

'Both,' she said. 'Bacon sarnie? It was always a tradition after a night shift.'

'You read my mind,' he said, and Megan could feel his eyes on her as she walked out of the room.

In the kitchen, she fed the cats first, knowing from experience that she was not going to be allowed to do anything else until that most important of jobs had been finished. Megan flicked the switches for the kettle and the grill, and waited for both to warm up. As she waited, her mind replayed the conversation they had had last night, rewinding back to the question he had asked her. Why did she think he had gone to the press? As her mind pressed the play button, she realised that he had not actually answered her own question: was it him?

She frowned, and then shook her head. It couldn't have been him. He'd said he had concerns about her ability to look after the cats, but that wasn't enough of a reason, surely? She put some rashers of bacon under the grill and pulled out the brown sauce from the fridge, wondering as she did if he were a red or a brown sauce man.

'Megan?' The voice from the lounge sounded urgent. Megan turned off the grill and dashed back in as quickly as her still-swollen toes would allow. In her fear she couldn't seem to form any words to ask what was wrong, and dread filled her stomach.

She looked from Doctor Wakefield to the sofa, and felt herself sag with relief. Old Man was sat up: he was swaying slightly, but she was sure she could make out a soft purr as the vet scratched behind his ears.

'Old Man,' Megan said, reaching out to stroke him, 'you had us so worried. Please don't ever do that again.'

She could feel the tears come again, but this time they were happy tears. Doctor Wakefield stood up and squeezed her shoulder.

'I'll give you two a minute, and go and finish fixing up breakfast'.

Megan sat beside Old Man on the sofa. To her surprise, he took a few uncertain steps, and then settled in her lap.

'It's okay,' she said softly. 'It's all going to be okay.'

Doctor Wakefield walked in to the room with a loaded tray, piled high with bacon sandwiches and steaming mugs of fresh coffee. Megan's tummy rumbled in appreciation and she was rewarded with a smile.

He sat next to her and handed her a sandwich. She bit into it, and brown sauce oozed out the sides and dribbled down her chin. She tried to surreptitiously wipe it away, but he laughed, and she knew she had been caught in the act.

'Hope you like brown sauce,' he said, and Megan wondered once again if he was a mind-reader. She nodded, mouth too full of delicious sandwich to answer.

'If you ask me, it's the only thing to have with bacon.'

Megan tried not to stare. How was it that the haughty, arrogant, totally-convinced-of-his-own-worth Doctor Wakefield had suddenly morphed into what to Megan was a near-perfect man? She shook her head gently, sternly reminding herself how tired she was, and how that could affect her perception of life in general. Doctor Wakefield, for his part, looked slightly bemused by the internal conversation that Megan was having with herself.

'I've taken some more bloods this morning,' he said, switching back to the most important person in the room at that moment. 'Keep him on water only until I get the results. I'll give you a ring later, and we can discuss how and when to reintroduce food.'

'I will. I'm not letting him out of my sight. I think we both deserve a quiet day indoors today.' She stroked Old Man gently, and felt his even breathing with relief. 'I can't let you out until I know you aren't going to do something foolish like drink antifreeze again!' She looked up at Doctor Wakefield, but the smile on her face froze as she saw his expression.

'What is it?' she asked, feeling the panic beginning to rise again. Had the vet spotted something that had him concerned for Old Man's recovery? 'You said you thought he would be fine!' She knew she sounded panicky, but she couldn't help it — fear and fatigue were a terrible mix.

'Megan,' Doctor Wakefield said in a

stern but caring way, 'I think Old Man is going to be fine. I need to run his bloods, but all the signs are good.' He seemed reluctant to continue, and Megan couldn't wait.

'So, what is it?'

He steepled his hands in front of his face and looked like he was trying to find the right words.

'Old Man doesn't go far these days,' he said, frowning at something that Megan couldn't work out.

'Not beyond the confines of the garden, no.' She rubbed her tired eyes, trying to make her brain work faster.

'And you haven't being doing anything with antifreeze?'

Megan snorted. She knew nothing about cars, and even had to take hers into the garage to get her oil and tyres checked.

'No chance,' she said. 'I don't know much about cars, but even I can work out that you probably don't need to worry about antifreeze in the summer . . . ' Her voice trailed away, and

Doctor Wakefield waited as her brain started to put the jigsaw together.

'So how did Old Man come across antifreeze?' Megan asked, her eyes widening as her thoughts raced. 'Graham and Chloe don't drive.' She felt the colour drain from her face as she contemplated a possible option. Could someone want rid of her so badly that they would poison one of Auntie Cath's beloved cats? She sat forward suddenly, making Old Man start; she quickly soothed him with a stroke. 'What about the other cats?' she asked, feeling panic and fear overwhelm her.

'I've already checked. They all seem fine, and the access to the pens is locked. Whoever did this couldn't get to them without breaking the padlock.'

'So they went for Old Man instead?' Megan could feel her panic replaced by cold, hard anger. 'How could anyone do that?' she demanded, her voice louder than she had intended.

'I don't know,' he said quietly, but he too seemed outraged. 'Telling tales to the press is one thing — hateful, yes — but poisoning an animal, that's criminal.'

He turned his face to her now.

'Megan, I think you need to report this to the police.'

19

Megan threw herself down on the sofa and closed her eyes. She didn't think she had ever felt so weary, and considering her experiences as a nurse, that was saying something. She was physically tired, but she was used to that — this was something else. Someone was targeting her, and she had no idea why. Targeting the business, as Doctor Wakefield had said, was one thing — but going after the cats was something entirely different.

She'd called the local police station, and the female beat officer had turned up an hour later. PC Taylor had taken the report seriously, and promised that she would look into it.

Megan wasn't sure if that made her feel better or worse. Part of her wanted the police officer to point out that it could all be an accident; but when

Megan had told her about the newspaper reports, PC Taylor's mouth had formed a grim line, and Megan couldn't shake the feeling that perhaps this wasn't the first incident of this kind in the village.

Megan had explained the events to Chloe and Graham, asking them to ensure all the gates to the cattery were always locked, and to keep a close eye out. They seemed in shock too, and even Graham had asked to be allowed to come and see Old Man. The cat, for his part, seemed none the worse for wear. Doctor Wakefield had called and said the blood tests showed no long-term damage, although he would repeat them in forty-eight hours just to be sure, and suggested that Megan feed Old Man on a light diet of white fish. Old Man had scoffed the lot and was now curled up on the sofa beside her. She reached out to stroke him, just to check he was okay, and then the doorbell rang.

Megan closed her eyes and hoped that whoever it was would simply go away. Then her mobile, which she had thrown on the coffee table, started to ring. She sighed, knowing that the chances of the two events being closely connected were pretty high. She reached a hand across to it and picked it up. *Greg* appeared on the front screen.

'Hello?' she said, not bothering to hide the tiredness from her voice.

'Megan, are you alright? I just heard.' He sounded worried.

'I'm fine, and Old Man is going to be okay. We're just exhausted,' she said, hoping that he might take the hint and leave her be and then wondering why she felt like that. She frowned, and then reminded herself that she was sleep-deprived.

'I'm sure you are. I'm on the doorstep. Didn't you hear the bell ring?'

Megan bit her tongue down on the retort that she knew was coming, along the lines of 'Why do people who have been up all night usually ignore the doorbell?' Before she could think of words to say that wouldn't offend

— after all, he was only being nice, wasn't he? — he said, 'Can I come in? I won't take long. I just want to check you are all alright.'

Megan held the handset away from her ear and stared at it, wondering if she was dreaming. He seemed to really want to see her, which was nice but he also seemed disproportionately worried about her — which, in her tired state, made her feel a little annoyed. She could look after herself.

She could hear muffled tones from the phone. 'Sorry, just coming,' she said, and rolled onto her feet, wincing as her toes hit the carpet. She shuffled along the hall and opened the door.

'You look awful,' he said, with no trace of irony.

She stepped back to let him in, since it seemed clear he was not going to leave her to sleep until he had established in his own mind that all was fine.

'Well, I haven't been to bed since I last saw you,' Megan said, but again

Greg didn't seem to pick up on the cue, and instead walked past her into the lounge.

'Feel free to make yourself at home,' Megan murmured to no one but herself, and then felt guilty that she was giving Greg a hard time since he was clearly showing concern for her. She took a deep breath and followed him into the lounge. She found him kneeling beside Old Man, peering at him as if he was trying to work out whether he was okay.

'He's fine, Greg, really. Doctor Wakefield said we caught it in time. His bloods are back to normal, and he just needs to take it easy for a few days.'

Once again, Megan wondered at his reaction; even though Greg had a cat of his own, he had never shown much interest in hers.

'Wakefield?' he asked sharply.

Megan nodded.

'I called him last night when I found Old Man. He looked after him all night,' she added, suddenly feeling like she should be defending the vet. Megan saw Greg relax a little. She knew there was history between the two, but still had the feeling that she was missing something important.

Megan sat down beside Old Man's basket, and so Greg was forced to either remain kneeling or sit in one of the armchairs opposite. He chose the former. She waited for him to speak, not knowing what to say. The atmosphere between them seemed different somehow, not the relaxed ease of their date but more like an awkward meeting of exes.

'Do you know how it happened?' Greg asked finally, leaning forward in his chair.

'No,' Megan said, looking at Old Man, feeling the need to break eye contact with Greg, 'but I got the impression from the police that it's not the first time something like this has occurred.'

'You called the police? That's a bit OTT, isn't it?' Greg asked, and Megan blinked. Two seconds ago he was all concerned, and now he seemed to think she was overreacting.

'Well, as Doctor Wakefield pointed out, poisoning an animal is a criminal offence,' Megan said stiffly, knowing that mentioning the vet again would get a rise out of Greg, but not really caring at that moment. She had no idea what was going on with Greg, but what she did know was that she was too tired to really care.

'Not if it was accidental, surely?' Greg said, aiming for a reasonable tone but not really managing it.

'It could have been accidental, but seems unlikely. It hasn't come from my car, and Graham and Chloe don't drive. Old Man doesn't wander further than the back garden, so it seems unlikely he came across it by accident.'

'But you'd rather think someone did it on purpose.'

Megan stared at him.

'No, of course not, but I think I have to at least explore the possibility that someone might have tried to poison the cats. What if they tried to do something else to them? I have to at least be careful.' Megan couldn't keep the annoyance from her voice. Why was he being like this?

Greg stood up abruptly.

'I can see you're tired. I'll let you get some sleep. Perhaps we can talk about this later.' And with that he left the room, and Megan heard the door close.

'What,' Megan said to Old Man, who pricked up one ear and opened an eye, 'was all that about?'

20

Megan's alarm clock was shrill, and she knocked it off the bedside table in her hurry to switch it off. She had been in a deep sleep, and the temptation to ignore it and roll over had been great. However, experience of coming off night shifts and needing to adjust to being awake in the daytime again had taught her not to sleep long on the day after her last night. If you did, you simply promised yourself a restless night of no sleep, and the cycle remained unbroken. She sat up, and her brain started to whirl with the events of the last few days. So much had happened, most of which she didn't understand. As if in response to this, a dull ache started to form behind her eyes, and so she made her way to the kitchen to make coffee.

A quick check on Old Man found

him fast asleep in his bed. He chirruped at her when she reached out to stroke his head, stretched, and then closed his eyes. Megan couldn't help but wish she could join him. She needed to stay awake so she would sleep tonight, and she needed to try and work out what was going on.

She grabbed a notepad that Auntie Cath kept by the landline, and a pen from the pot, then made her way back to the kitchen. She wrote down *Front-page news*, then *Old Man*, then *Who would know?*, and then finally *Why!*. She sat and stared at the words, letting her mind wander, hoping it would come up with some plausible explanation.

She turned over the page and wrote *Doctor Wakefield*. After their first meeting, she could have believed he would speak to the papers, and Greg's experiences with him seemed to uphold that theory. But from what she had seen of him since, it just didn't seem to fit. She scribbled *Wants to buy the business?.* That was Greg's suggestion, but Megan was still unsure. She couldn't see *why* he would want it. It just didn't seem to make sense. If he had the money to buy it, then he could probably just set up his own cattery — no doubt a much posher affair than Cath's Cats — and compete with her for customers.

Megan leaned back in her chair and took a sip of coffee. One thing she knew for absolute certain was that he would never harm an animal, whatever his business aspirations might be. So did that mean that there were two people in the village who wanted her out? She idly wrote down *Old Man was poisoned*, but there was no way to connect those dots, and she knew deep down that he could not possibly have been involved.

Who else would have a motive? She wrote *Graham*, simply because she couldn't think of anyone else; but again she couldn't see him talking to anyone, let alone poisoning Old Man. She threw the pen down. Maybe she should leave the detective work to the professionals. PC Taylor had said she would look into it, and she presumably had the skills and local knowledge to do a better job than Megan could.

She sighed; she couldn't do anything about the mystery person, but she could focus on the business and the welfare of all the cats. She pushed herself up from the chair and headed in the direction of the shower. Hopefully that would wake her up a bit, and then she could get to work.

Megan was just triple-checking the outer door lock to the cattery when her phone beeped in her pocket.

I would like to come and check in on Old Man after surgery this evening. I should be with you around seven. Please let me know if this is not convenient.

Megan couldn't help but smile that his professional manner was back. She shook her head; Doctor Wakefield was really a person of two halves.

Seven will be fine, she sent back. *Would you like to stay to dinner? As a thank-you?* she added quickly, and then pressed *Send* before she could edit all of the last two sentences out. What was she doing? An image of Greg came into her mind. Was she being disloyal? No, she told herself firmly, it was just a thank-you dinner — nothing more. Despite those words to herself, she hurried indoors to pick up the keys so she could head to the supermarket to buy something nice to cook which would also give her enough time to get changed.

* * *

It was all a bit of a rush to get ready. The spaghetti bolognese was bubbling softly on the stove, and the garlic bread was ready to go in. She had just changed into something that didn't smell of cats, and done her hair: all she needed to do was lay the kitchen table.

The doorbell chimed. She would

have to lay the table whilst Doctor Wakefield was here — but that was fine, she told herself: it wasn't like she was on a date.

She pulled open the door, and it was clear that she hadn't been the only one to get changed. Doctor Wakefield was dressed in dark navy chinos and a red t-shirt which fitted his body well. He looked like he had just leapt out of the shower himself, as his hairline was still damp. He smiled at her, and Megan swallowed. *Not a date*, she told herself, suspecting that it was going to become her mantra.

'How's the patient?' he asked

'He seems to be doing fine. He's drinking plenty of water, and managed a little fish.' Megan gestured for him to follow her. 'I really appreciate all you have done, Doctor Wakefield.'

'Will, please,' he said. 'You don't work for me,' he added with a smile of explanation. Turning his attention to his patient, he reached into his leather equipment bag for a stethoscope, listening to Old

Man's heart and lungs before checking his pulse.

'All looks good,' Will said, looking up at her. 'A few more days of quiet and fish diet, and he should be back to his old self.'

Megan relaxed and let out her held-in breath. A small part of her had been holding onto the fear that Old Man's recovery had been too smooth to be true. Then Will was standing in front of her, one arm reaching out for hers. He waited until she looked up at him — she had never really realised before quite how tall he was.

'He is fine, Megan. I promise.'

Megan nodded, not knowing what to say, and not wanting to cry with relief again.

'Come on through. I need to put the garlic bread in the oven. Perhaps you could pour the wine?'

Megan led the way to the kitchen and handed him the bottle. She turned her attention to the pan on the stove before opening the oven door and popping the garlic bread on the shelf.

'Be ready in about ten minutes,' she said, turning with a smile that froze on her face. Will had opened and poured the wine, but he was now staring at something on the kitchen table. Megan felt like all of the breath had been knocked out of her as she realised that she had left the notebook open there.

'Will . . . ' she started, but his look made the words die on his lips.

'You think I could have poisoned Old Man?' His voice was incredulous, but the pain was written all across his face.

'No!' Megan said, so hurriedly that it came out as a shout. 'Exactly the opposite. I know you couldn't have.' She tried to pour all her belief in that fact into her words, but she knew she had already lost the battle. Will was shaking his head in disbelief.

'If you could even consider the possibility . . . ' He didn't need to finish the sentence. Megan knew all was lost. He might have forgiven her for almost anything else, but his love for animals was such a core part of him that to question it was unforgiveable.

He seemed to remember where he was. 'I think I'd better go,' he said, and put down the glass of untouched wine.

'Please don't. Let me explain,' Megan said, crossing the room towards him, but he took a step away from her.

'Thank you for the kind offer of dinner, but I'm afraid I will have to decline.'

He looked at her one more time, and Megan didn't think it was possibly to feel any more wretched. She wanted to find something to say that would make him understand, that would stop him leaving, but she could think of nothing.

When the tears came this time, she didn't bother to try and stop them. The front door shut and she was alone, and she couldn't help but think she had lost something terribly precious.

21

Megan didn't know what time she had fallen asleep, but she knew she had been crying when sleep finally claimed her. Her eyes felt gritty, and one look in the mirror told her they were puffy too. There was only one thing for it. She knew herself well enough to know that moping never helped: she needed to get to work. Consequentially, she was in the office before Chloe, who started a little in surprise.

'Morning,' Megan said, forcing herself to at least appear cheerful. 'We've a busy day ahead. Three going home and four coming in. Hopefully no one will cancel. Tea?' She wasn't keen to chat, so filling in any quiet spaces seemed like a plan.

'Please.' Chloe said. 'Have you seen the paper this morning?' she asked, and Megan felt her heart drop. Surely not again!

'No,' she said, keeping her back to Chloe as she made the tea, not sure she could control her emotions if it was more bad news.

'Little River Primary is in the county finals for netball!' Chloe said, sounding so excited that Megan wondered if she had misheard, and in fact they had qualified for the Olympics.

'That's great,' Megan said, turning around and offering Chloe a cup. 'No mention of Cath's Cats, then?' she added, knowing that she couldn't put it off any longer.

'Only the usual advert,' Chloe said, and Megan felt some of the tension leave her shoulders. That, at least, was a relief. An image of Will's hurt face swam into her mind, but she pushed it firmly away. She had no idea what she could do to repair the damage she had done, and obsessing about it hadn't helped, so all she could do was hope that by not thinking about it, her mind would come up with a plan.

'Old Man's at his usual post,' Chloe

remarked as she went through to where they kept the cleaning tools and food.

Megan smiled. Old Man sat in his usual window spot had been the first positive thing that had happened that morning. Maybe it was an omen that things were only going to get better.

'Doctor Wakefield coming to check on him today?' Chloe asked

'I don't think so,' Megan managed to say, although she felt her throat had closed up.

'That must mean he's well and truly on the mend,' Chloe said, loading up her trolley with all the different types of cat food the picky residents ate. 'One thing you can say about Doctor Wakefield is that he loves his animals.' With that, Chloe pushed the trolley out of the office, and left Megan to her thoughts.

She tried to do some deep breathing, but it was no good. The memories of the night before came back in shame-inducing detail.

The door opened.

'Megan? What's wrong? Is it Old Man?' a familiar voice asked. And before Megan could reply, she found herself pulled into the open arms of Greg.

In that moment, Megan clung on to Greg like a lifejacket in a stormy sea. Perhaps Greg would say something, anything, that could ease the terrible weight she felt in her chest. When she had calmed a little, she eased herself out of his grip and sat back on the chair. Greg, for his part, rolled over another chair so that he could sit next to her.

'I was trying to work out who might be trying to attack the business, and who might have tried to poison Old Man. I was just scribbling thoughts in a notebook, and I left it out on the side. Will saw it and got really upset.'

Megan winced at the memory of his face, so hurt and offended.

'Are you sure it wasn't guilt?' Greg said thoughtfully as he leaned back in his chair. 'Maybe he was upset that you had caught him out?'

Megan shook her head fiercely. If nothing else, she knew deep down that Will would never hurt an animal.

'I know you don't like him — '

Before she could continue, Greg cut her off. 'With good reason,' he said pointedly.

Megan waved her hands, not wanting to go over old ground. 'Yes, I know all that,' she said impatiently, 'but when I thought about it, I couldn't imagine he would hurt an animal. He just wouldn't.'

'Unless he knew he would be close by to swoop in and save the day,' Greg said darkly. '*Will* seems to have won you over.'

'He saved Old Man's life,' Megan said, responding in kind.

'I know that,' Greg said with an exaggerated sigh, 'but that doesn't mean he wasn't the reason for Old Man being sick in the first place.'

Megan frowned. This conversation was not going the way she had hoped; it certainly wasn't comforting or reassuring in any way. 'I think we should stop discussing this since it's clear we aren't going to agree.'

'I'm sorry,' Greg said, reaching out a hand to rest on her arm. 'I can see you're upset, and I'm not helping. It's just that I know Wakefield better than you do, and I would hate you to be taken in by his routine of charming, animal-loving country vet.'

Megan bristled and moved her hand away.

'And I've done it again, haven't I?' Greg said with a rueful smile. 'Let me make it up to you? There's a folk band playing in the pub tonight. How about I treat you to dinner and some live music?'

Megan studied his expression, which seemed so genuine, and remembered the fun that they'd had on their previous date. Was she really willing to ruin two friendships in one day just because she was feeling upset and cross?

'Okay,' she said. 'Maybe just for an hour or two. I don't want to leave Old

Man alone for too long.'

'Great,' Greg said, his smile now broad. 'I'll pick you up at seven?'

Megan shook her head. 'I think I'll walk down, thanks — my toes are feeling better and I need the exercise. But I'll meet you there at seven.'

Greg looked as if he were going to argue, but then thought better of it.

'I'll see you later,' he said, and leaned over for a kiss. At the last minute, Megan turned her face away, so it turned into a peck on the cheek. They locked eyes for a moment — Greg's showing a little hurt, and something else — and then he smiled as if to show he understood, before walking away and closing the door behind him. Leaving Megan feeling more confused than ever.

Megan spent the rest of the day focusing all her energy on work. Her conversation with Greg had left her even more conflicted about her feelings and what was going on. There was something about Greg's reaction to Will that didn't ring true. It seemed childish to her, however much you had been hurt in business, to assume that a vet would harm a pet on purpose. She couldn't work out his reaction — unless he was jealous, of course; but that seemed ridiculous since they had only been going out together briefly. She had thought about ringing him to cancel the evening, to give her more time to think, but was again reminded that she had ruined one budding friendship in the last twenty-four hours and couldn't afford to lose another.

It was a warm evening, and walking down through the village lifted her spirits a little. Auntie Cath had been right about living in the country: Megan was growing to love it, and wasn't missing London at all. She was navigating a small stretch of lane when she heard a car pull up behind her. A glance over her shoulder told her that it was Will, the front of his Range Rover emblazoned with the veterinary clinic's logo. She slowed her walking to a stop, curious, but also a little nervous that she might be in for another scolding.

'Megan,' he said. She took that as a good sign that he hadn't defaulted back to 'Miss Falstaff'.

'Will, hi,' she said, and tried a small smile. It wasn't returned, and his face was serious — she wondered if he was about to give her bad news. The thought that perhaps there was a worrying update about Old Man made her sway a little, and she had to reach out for the wound-down window to steady herself.

'Are you okay?' he asked, suddenly concerned.

Megan nodded. 'Fine,' she mumbled. 'Is it Old Man?'

He frowned, looking confused. 'No, unless he has deteriorated?'

Megan shook her head. 'He seems fine to me.'

Will nodded slowly, and it was clear to Megan that they were talking at cross-purposes.

'Sorry, when you stopped, I thought

perhaps you had new results on him, and it was bad news.'

Will's face seemed to resolve into understanding. 'It's not about Old Man, but I do have some news for you.' His face was grim, and so Megan knew immediately that it wasn't good.

22

Megan stared and said nothing. Again, she felt like the rest of the world knew what was going on and she didn't.

'Do you want to get in?' Will said. 'I can drop you to wherever you are going and tell you on the way.'

His manner was giving nothing away, and Megan had to admit she was now intensely curious to know what was going on, so she opened the car door and climbed in. Inside was a mix you would expect from a successful vet. The fabric was all leather and high-spec, but the floor carpet showed signs of his profession with clumps of mud and straw. She couldn't help but smile, then remembered all that had happened and made her face neutral. She glanced up to see that Will was looking at her curiously, but there was no evidence of anger.

'Where are you headed?' Will asked, driving off.

'The pub,' Megan replied. 'There's a folk band playing, and I'm going to meet Greg.'

Will was silent in response.

'Is that a problem?' she asked, trying to keep her voice even, and wondering if her friend had been right, that men complicate life.

'That depends on what you make of what I have to tell you.' Will said cryptically.

'Okay,' Megan said slowly, wondering if this was going to be his side of the Will-Greg business issue.

Will took a deep breath and kept his eyes firmly fixed on the road ahead.

'I've been thinking about what you said the other night.'

Megan opened her mouth to try and apologise again, but Will held up a staying hand.

'Not that part,' he said, and Megan felt her shoulders relax a little. 'I was thinking about who might have an

196

interest in ruining your business.'

He glanced at her, and she nodded to show she was listening.

'So I asked a friend of mine in the council's planning department — ' Megan filed that piece of information away to think about later. ' — and she told me that there is a planning application in its early stages for the field behind the cattery.'

'Okay,' Megan said, not able to put the pieces together.

'Apparently, concerns have been raised by the planning committee about access to the site. The plans are for luxury apartments, so multiple-occupancy, and that means traffic. Debra thinks that unless the applicant can resolve the access issue, the plans will be rejected.'

Megan closed her eyes. She had a feeling that she knew where this was going, but needed Will to say it.

'The company that has submitted the plans is Ford Construction.'

Megan swallowed.

'That's Greg Ford.'

For a moment, Megan didn't know how she felt, and then her emotions hit her like a battering ram. Anger, hurt, embarrassment at being taken in; and mortification that Will had been the one to figure it out when she had seemingly been blinded by a charming smile.

'I'm sorry,' Will said. 'I know you like him.'

'I don't really know him,' she replied through gritted teeth. 'But how . . . ' She wondered how Greg had done it. She was expecting Will to take up the story, but his eyes remained firmly fixed on the road in front, as if he didn't want to look her in the eye.

'Will? I know there's something else, so you may as well just tell me.' She braced herself for what other information he had.

'I phoned up the paper and asked for information on their lead reporter. I did a little digging on the internet and found the connection to Ford.'

'Which is?' Megan said softly, not sure that she wanted to know the answer.

'I found the reporter's social media page. There are lots of photos of her together with Greg. I'm sorry, Megan, but it would appear they are boyfriend and girlfriend.'

Humiliation blossomed in Megan's chest. How had she been to easily taken in? How had she not seen through him? Had this man whom she had trusted actually tried to kill Old Man? And then blamed it on Will, the person she had falsely accused, and possibly ruined her friendship with him forever . . .

In a sudden, surprising rush, Megan burst into tears. Will seemed unfazed by this. He simply drove to the next farm gate and pulled the car in. He undid his seatbelt, then Megan's, and pulled her into his arms.

'I'm so sorry, Megan. I really am. I didn't want to hurt you, but I felt in all good conscience I couldn't keep this information to myself. I'm sorry.'

'Don't be,' Megan sobbed. 'It all makes sense now. I feel like such an idiot.' She wailed, 'And you think I think you poisoned Old Man!' The thought of that made her body shake with the shame, and she felt Will's arms pull her tighter to his chest.

'I should have stayed and listened to you,' he said softly into her hair, 'I have a short fuse, and I've let it get in the way too many times.'

'Greg tried to tell me it was you, but I couldn't believe it, I wouldn't,' Megan said.

'I guess he needed to shift the blame onto someone; and after our first encounter, I suppose he found a suitable target.'

'He also said something about business,' Megan said, feeling that the time was right to get everything out in the open.

'I bet he did,' Will said ruefully. 'Probably quite a different version to the one I would tell you.'

'I believe you,' Megan added fiercely.

'You don't have to be so quick; you haven't even heard my side yet,' Will said, a faint chuckle rising in his chest.

'That man tried to kill my cat!' Megan spat, and the thought of it made the tears rise up in her again.

'We don't know that he actually did it,' Will said, his reasonableness chiming another chord within Megan. How had she trusted Greg, who was so full of malice towards Will, over him? 'We know he is involved, but accusing him of something criminal with no evidence — well, that's probably not very fair.'

Megan shifted in his arms, but didn't want to pull away. She felt safe and secure for the first time in a while, and wasn't ready to give that up just yet.

'I don't feel like being fair,' she grumbled. 'If you hadn't been there, then Old Man . . . ' She let her voice trail off, not able to finish the thought out loud: it was too painful.

'Megan, Old Man is going to be fine,' Will said. 'The police are looking into the poisoning.'

'But what if he tries again?' The thought made Megan shiver.

'Well, I was thinking that a little

public discussion of the subject might persuade him, if he was involved, to steer clear. What do you think?'

Now Megan did pull herself away. And it might have been her overactive, needy imagination, but she could have sworn Will was as reluctant as her to break the embrace.

'I think that sounds like an excellent plan.'

Will cocked his head to one side. 'It's handy that we know we'll find him in the most public spot in Little River, then, isn't it.' His eyes flashed, and Megan nodded.

There was no parking at the pub: obviously the live music night was popular with local residents and visitors alike. Will found a spot further up the little high street that ran through the centre. Megan yanked open the car door and started to stride off in the direction of the pub. A hand caught her and swung her round, and she found herself back in Will's arms.

'Megan,' he said, a warning tone in

his voice, 'remember that we have no evidence that Greg was involved in Old Man's poisoning.'

'We have to stop him,' she said, leaning back so she could see his face.

'We don't know it was him; but if not, then the chances are that there is someone else in the pub who was involved. We need to give a general warning, not go about attacking individuals.'

'*He's* attacking *me*!' she said indignantly. 'He's been telling his reporter girlfriend all sorts of stories about the cattery, trying to run me out of business. *And* — ' She paused for effect. ' — he didn't tell me he had a girlfriend!'

Will considered her for a few moments, holding her close as if he was worried that she would run off.

'Maybe I should go by myself.' His tone was serious, but Megan was sure she could detect a hint of amusement.

'Are you saying I can't control myself?' she enquired, eyebrow arched.

'Based on current evidence, I have my doubts.' And this time he lost the battle with his face, and grinned. 'Sorry,' he said when he saw her mutinous expression, 'I know you must be hurt by all of this, but it won't make you feel better to get slapped with a defamation of character suit.'

Some of Megan's anger faded. He was right, of course — which was surprisingly annoying.

'Fine,' she said, 'you can do the talking. I'll just watch.'

A car screeched up beside them, and Megan recognised it at once.

'Hey! Get your hands off her!' Greg yelled, not even bothering to shut his car door.

23

Megan felt an unexpected stab of guilt, which she quickly pushed aside. As if she had anything to feel guilty about!

'I don't think this is any of your business,' Will said in an icy-cool voice.

'Manhandling my girlfriend is my business!' Greg hissed through gritted teeth. He turned his attention to Megan. 'Do you want me to call the police'

Megan almost laughed out loud. Greg was still under the impression that he hadn't been found out.

'Which girlfriend would that be, Ford?' Will asked, his tone still cool. 'Megan, or the lead reporter for the local rag?'

Greg froze, and his expression seemed stuck in angry indignation.

'It's not what you think,' Greg said suddenly, turning his attention back to Megan.

'Really?' she said, surprised at her

own calm, 'So you don't have a girlfriend?' He opened his mouth to speak, but Megan held up an imperious hand before stepping out of Will's arms. 'You don't want to buy the land that my business is on? You haven't been getting your girlfriend to vilify me in the press?' She watched as he struggled to keep up with the revelations. 'I bet you don't even *have* a cat.' She barked out a laugh — this was the thing that finally made him blush!

'I've been to the police, you know.' Her tone was quiet, but the implication was not lost on Greg.

'I had nothing to do with Old Man's poisoning I swear.' Greg said urgently, and Megan felt swayed for a moment — but only a moment when she remembered how easily he had lied to her about everything else.

'Why should I believe you?' she asked, and felt Will's hand on her arm.

'As you said, Megan, the police are investigating. No doubt they will find out the truth and deal with those involved,' Will said. 'Now, I think we should go.' He turned his face to Megan, and they exchanged looks.

'It wasn't all a lie,' Greg said as Megan and Will turned to get back in the car.

She looked back at him.

'My feelings for you are real, Megan.'

Will shook his head at this last-ditch attempt.

'I'll prove it to you — '

If he had attempted to say anything else, his words were cut off as Megan slammed the door. Will put the car in gear and drove off slowly around Greg and his abandoned vehicle. Megan willed herself not to, but just as they were driving out of sight, she looked back. Greg was leaning against the car with his hands in his pockets, staring at the ground. Whether it was because his plans had been foiled or he had been speaking the truth, Megan couldn't tell.

She leaned back in the seat, feeling suddenly exhausted.

'Are you okay?' Will asked after a few

minutes' silence.

Megan nodded, too tired to speak.

'I'll drop you home. You look done in.'

Megan turned to him with a grateful smile.

'Have you eaten anything? I could rustle us up some pasta,' he said, gesturing over his shoulder to the shopping bag that Megan hadn't seen earlier. She took a few moments to weigh up her hunger versus her desire to go to bed and forget about everything for a while. She looked across at Will, who was again concentrating on the road — giving her time to think, she was sure — and that made up her mind.

'That would be lovely.'

★   ★   ★

Later, Megan mentally added 'good cook' to Will's list of talents. He had cooked a fresh sauce from scratch, and even cleaned up after himself as he went. Another positive in Megan's book.

'How are you feeling?' Will asked, bringing the conversation back to the elephant in the room that they had managed to avoid although dinner.

'Confused,' Megan said honestly, casting a quick look in Will's direction to gauge his reaction. Will's face gave away nothing: he simply nodded.

'I mean, I know he was behind the newspaper reports, and I know he was trying to run me out of business — but would he really poison one of my cats?' She shook her head at the thought.

Will's face showed relief, and she thought she knew why; she gave him a little smile. 'You thought I was confused about something else?'

Will shrugged, trying to act nonchalant but not succeeding. 'I know he can be persuasive. I was a little concerned you had been taken in.'

'Once bitten, twice shy,' Megan said in response as the doorbell rang.

They exchanged glances. It was clear

that they both had their suspicions as to who would be ringing the doorbell at gone eleven at night.

'Do you want me to go?' Will asked. Megan sighed.

'No, I should,' she said as hauled herself off of the sofa. She was really not in the mood for any more drama.

She composed her face and opened the door. As predicted, Greg was standing on the step.

'I know I have no right to ask you to listen to what I have to say . . . ' He held up both hands, palms towards her. Megan raised an eyebrow. 'But I think you will want to hear what I have to tell you.'

Megan let the words sit in the air for a moment, and then nodded.

'I know who poisoned Old Man.'

Now Megan's eyes narrowed as she wondered if once again he would try and lay the blame at Will's feet.

'It was Abigail. Abigail Curan.'

'Your girlfriend?' Megan's voice had moved up a notch, and she could hear

Will moving into the hall behind her. 'You had your girlfriend try to kill my cat!' She pulled her mobile phone out from her pocket, intending to ring the police.

'You don't need to call the police,' Greg said.

Megan narrowed her eyes. If he thought a confession was going to stop her, he had another think coming.

'All I mean is, you don't *need* to. I've already done it. I had my suspicions before, and so I checked the satnav in her car. The last journey was to your bungalow, and I found the antifreeze in the boot. I've given all the evidence to the police.'

Megan stared, not knowing what to say.

'Are seriously trying to tell Megan that you knew nothing about this?' Will said, his voice sounding from over Megan's shoulder.

'Stay out of it!' he shouted in Will's direction before turning his attention back to Megan. 'I swear I didn't know. I would have stopped her. All I asked her to do was to write some pieces for the paper. She agreed, and once she started getting noticed in the paper, she was happy to continue.'

'Even if you didn't ask her to . . . ' Megan said, her voice trailing off.

'Don't you see?' He looked at her now, and his eyes were wide and pleading. 'She had worked out that I had fallen in love with you. She'd said as much to me before, but I never thought she would do something to hurt you, hurt Old Man. Please, Megan, I know I've made mistakes, but my feelings are true. I realised that tonight. I can't lose you — please let me try and explain.'

Megan was suddenly aware of Will's presence behind her. She was a mess of emotions, and so tired she didn't know which way was up. Before she could formulate her answer, Will butted in.

'You don't seriously buy what he is telling you?' Will's voice was incredulous, and Megan knew that the flare of anger she felt towards him in that moment was unfair, but somehow she couldn't suppress it. It was not up to Will who she talked to.

When she made no reply, Megan heard him walk back into the kitchen. A moment later he was back at the door with his jacket in his hand.

'I think I'd better go,' he said. Greg stepped out of the way, unable to keep the relief from his face. Will looked at him stonily, glanced back at Megan, and then was gone.

24

'Now he's gone, maybe we can have a proper conversation.'

Megan tore her eyes away from Will's car as it drove off, looking back to Greg. She wasn't sure if she was ready to — or even wanted to — hear what he had to say.

'I know I have a lot of explaining to do,' Greg said, trying out a smile. Megan didn't smile back. What she needed was time to think everything through. It was all so confused in her mind. Her feelings for Greg had seemed so real. Did he deserve another chance, at least a chance to explain his side of things? Megan wasn't sure. She believed firmly in forgiveness and second chances, but still . . .

'Can I come in?' he asked hopefully, and Megan saw the Greg that she had fallen for on their first meeting. She stood back and let him walk past her.

Not being able to decide what she wanted to say, she threw herself down on the sofa and gestured for Greg to take a seat.

'I'm an idiot,' he said, and Megan didn't feel the need to disagree. 'I know I've hurt you with the newspaper thing, and I'm sorry. That all started before I met you, and as soon as I had, I regretted it. I tried to get Abby to stop, but she wouldn't'

Megan frowned.

'So you're saying that it would have been an okay thing to do to someone you didn't know and maybe didn't like?' The pieces were starting to fall into place in her head, and she thought she was beginning to see the real Greg.

'No, I'm not excusing it,' he said hurriedly. 'It's just business, you know how it is.'

Megan thought about this for a moment. 'Was the clinic issue *just business?*'

Greg's face darkened. 'I've told you

before, you don't want to go believing everything William Wakefield tells you.'

'That's just it,' Megan said. 'I do believe him. He tells me the truth. He tells me the truth even when it could hurt me.'

She paused and looked at Greg.

'Even when it could hurt him, or hurt what he wants.'

Megan's sleep-deprived brain was starting to make connections.

'But I love you,' Greg blurted out, as if that would make everything alright. 'I made some terrible mistakes and I'm sorry. If you give me a chance I will make it up to you.'

Megan studied his face.

'And what about the planning application? The need for access? I know all about it,' she said with a raised eyebrow.

Greg seemed to need a moment to formulate an answer.

'We can talk about that another time,' he said hopefully. 'Right now, we need to talk about us.'

Megan shook her head.

'But it affects us, Greg. That's the bit that you don't understand.'

'It doesn't have to,' he said firmly. 'Business and relationships should never mix. And it's not like your life's goal was to run a cattery.'

Megan froze.

'In a year's time, you would be selling it anyway. If you sell it to me, then we all win.'

Despite all the evidence that had presented to Megan, she knew something to be true in that moment. She didn't know Greg at all. She had thought she knew him, or at least was getting to know him. The way he thought and acted were so alien to her that she was sure they could never have a relationship — even if she could have forgiven and forgotten all that had happened to this point.

Greg seemed to realise that he was losing her. He moved to kneel beside the sofa, just as Will had done.

'Megan, please. I love you, I do. I

want you in my life. I can change, I promise I can.'

Megan looked in to his eyes, but her heart was made up. She knew that now. It seemed strange to her that it had taken so much to happen to reach this obvious conclusion.

'I know that you think you love me, Greg, but the fact is that you love someone who doesn't exist.' He opened his mouth to speak, but she held up a hand. 'I thought I loved you too, but I think we were both in love with the idea of each other. We are too different, you and I. I apply the same rules in life as in my business, and you don't.'

'I know you are angry with me right now, but isn't it worth giving us a chance?'

Megan sighed.

'You are missing the point, Greg. There is no 'us', except perhaps in our imaginations. I'm not the person for you, and you aren't the right person for me. I'm sorry,' she added as pain showed in his eyes. Even that did not make her change her mind; she knew the decision was right for both of them, and could only hope that one day Greg would understand that.

Greg stood up.

'You're tired,' he said. 'I should never have pushed to have this conversation now. Let's do dinner tomorrow night when we are both feeling better.'

Megan stood too, and reached out a hand.

'This was going to happen at some point. At some time in the future you would have realised that I'm not the person you want or need me to be.'

'Perhaps I'm realising that right now,' he said, not trying to keep the bitterness from his voice. 'If this is your way of punishing me for my mistakes, then you need to understand now that if I leave tonight with things as they are, there is no turning back. I'm not that kind of man.'

'It's not punishment, Greg! I was angry with you, of course I was. But that's not what this is about. It's like everything has suddenly become clear. We aren't right for each other, and no matter how much we might want to change, we won't be able to — worse, we would end up resenting each other.'

'And I supposed William Wakefield has helped with that clarity, has he?' It was said quietly, but Megan could still detect the sneer.

'This is not about him, Greg. It's about who you are and who I am. I wish that you could see that,' she added sadly. It wasn't as if she had thought this conversation would be friendly, but she hated to see him like this. Despite all that he had done, she didn't want to hurt him. She believed that he was genuinely sorry for what had happened to Old Man, and she also could see that he believed he loved her, but she knew for sure now how she felt.

'Keep telling yourself that, Megan, when you run back into his arms. Keep telling yourself that I'm the one who hurt you.' He looked at her now, and the pain in his face caused a similar reaction in herself. 'But right now, what you are doing, what you have done, is just as bad. You might like to think that we are different, but at least I have been honest with you about your mistakes.'

Megan stayed where she was and watched him leave, collapsing back onto the sofa when she heard the door close behind him.

25

However hard she tried to move on, Megan's brain insisted on replaying her last conversation with Greg. It wasn't that she had changed her mind. She knew deep down that a relationship with him would never work, but she hated to cause anyone pain, and it played on her mind. She turned over the words in her head and wondered if his comments about Will had been right. She was desperate to go and see Will, to tell him all that had happened, and see if they could be friends. In truth, she wanted to be more than friends — but she would settle for having him in her life in any way that he wanted. But she couldn't quite bring herself to re-establish contact with Will. She didn't want to cause Greg more pain, despite all that he had caused her — that was not her way. And part of her, she knew, was afraid. What if Will rejected her? She couldn't really blame him, since she had accused him of the worst thing in his eyes.

She padded around the bungalow a bit like a caged animal, not able to think of much else, and unable to concentrate on anything that might bring a welcome distraction. Nothing new had appeared in the papers. Megan wondered if Greg was behind that, or if Abigail had taken the sensible decision to stop — particularly since Megan was sure that the police would have, at the very least, had words with her.

The back door crashed open. 'Megan!'

Megan sighed. It was not so much that the distraction wasn't welcome — it was more that she was wondering what disaster had befallen them now.

'In here, Chloe. Everything alright?'

Chloe dashed into the lounge where Megan had been pacing, with a look of slight panic. 'It's Major Tom,' she said, slightly out of breath.

'Okay,' Megan said, putting her

hands on Chloe's shoulders so that she sat down, and worrying that she was going to have some sort of panic attack — either that, or faint. 'Take a breath, then tell me what's happened.'

'I think he's tried to get to space like his namesake.'

Megan blinked and tried to work out what was actually happening from those confusing words.

'Course, he doesn't have a spaceship,' Chloe added with a small frown, as if spaceships for cats were an actual thing.

'Chloe,' Megan said slowly, 'where is Major Tom right now?'

'Well, I think he thinks it's some kind of launchpad,' Chloe said, eyes wide.

Megan decided to take a deep breath of her own. 'And where would that be?' she asked, forcing the irritation from her voice.

'He's tried to climb up the side of the pen and he's got stuck.'

Megan nodded. Okay. That, at least, made sense. She started to walk towards the door; Chloe stood and followed her.

'Have you tried to coax him down?' Megan asked, feeling that this was a sensible suggestion, and therefore quite possibly one that Chloe hadn't considered.

'He's pretty cross,' Chloe said. 'I tried talking to him, but I think he's just crushed with disappointment that he's failed in his mission.'

Megan nodded her head slowly, wondering once more how Auntie Cath had coped with all the eccentricities that came with running a cattery.

'But don't worry!' Chloe said brightly. 'I called Doctor Wakefield, and he said he'd be right over.'

'I'm sure we can get Major Tom unstuck ourselves,' Megan said, hoping she would have time to ring and say everything was sorted. She ran a hand through hair she knew was a mess without needing a mirror. She was torn between badly wanting to see him, and not feeling ready to find out how he felt.

Chloe shook her head sadly.

'Major Tom will listen to Doctor Wakefield. I don't think he is in the mood to listen to us.'

Once they were outside and in the pens, Chloe gestured to a large longhair cat with tabby markings. Somehow he had managed to climb up the inside of the pen, wiggle through the tiniest of gaps, and then slip down between the inner chicken-wire fence and outer wooden fence. He looked to Megan to be unharmed. He also looked extremely surly. The low grumble in his throat got louder with every step Megan took; as she reached out a hand, he hissed so viciously that she found herself stumbling backwards.

'He does seem very cross,' Megan observed.

'So would you be if you managed to get yourself in that position.'

Megan didn't have to turn round to know who the voice belonged to. She took a minute to compose herself, then turned around with a small smile.

'Thanks for coming,' she said. 'We

seemed to have got ourselves into another scrape.'

Will nodded, but his eyes seemed fixed on Major Tom.

'I'm guessing Cathleen didn't warn you of the mischief that felines can get up to, then?'

Megan shook her head. Auntie Cath had told her stories of course, but she'd seemed to find them amusing rather than worrying.

'I just don't know how he did it,' Megan said, feeling like she should spend more time in the cattery and less time pacing and dwelling on things that she couldn't figure out.

'Turn your back for a second and they get up to all sorts. Just like children,' Will said, checking out the two layers of fencing. 'I think the safest way is going to be to cut the wire lower down and see if he can wiggle himself free. Of course, it means you will then have repairs to do . . . '

'That's fine,' Megan said hurriedly. 'Let's just get him out of there. He seems very unhappy in his predicament.'

Will nodded, then reached into his bag for some wire cutters. Megan was surprised that he had come equipped, and wondered if this wasn't the first animal he had had to rescue. She watched as he made his way towards the fence, saying nothing, but making eye contact with Major Tom. The cat hissed, and then meowed in a sorrowful way.

'Silly old boy,' Will said softly, and then proceeded to cut a cat-sized hole in the chicken-wire a little way down.

Ten minutes later, and Major Tom has shown no signs of budging. Will had made the hole wider in the hopes that would encourage him; but apart from the occasional hiss, the cat seemed happier to stay where he was rather than attempt to move. Will sat back on his heels, and seemed to ponder the situation.

'Chloe, have you got any chicken you could rustle up?'

Chloe nodded, and then dashed off in the direction of the office, calling: 'It's in the freezer, so will take me a few minutes.'

All the while that Chloe had been with them, they had been forced to focus on Major Tom. But now that she was gone, Megan felt like there was an elephant in the room. She wasn't sure what to say, but knew she needed to say *something*, since Will had shown no inclination to ask her.

'About the other night . . . ' Megan started.

'Its fine, Megan. It's your business. You don't need to worry about what I think.'

Megan frowned in irritation; the passive-aggressive thing did not go down well with her.

'Do you want to know what happened?' she demanded, not bothering to hide how cross she felt.

'If you want to tell me,' Will said casually, as if she had offered to tell him about her last holiday abroad and he really wasn't that bothered.

Megan sighed, and it was then Will turned to face her. He seemed to study her for a few moments.

'Sorry,' he said simply with a shrug. 'I guess I was a little hurt that you seemed to want to hear his side after everything that had happened.'

Megan moved so that she was sat beside him on the floor of the pen.

'You're right. I did want to hear what Greg had to say. I felt it was only right.'

Will nodded, but didn't look as if he agreed. Megan blew out her held-in breath; she wasn't explaining this very well.

'Greg and I had been out together.'

Will nodded, but kept his eyes focused on Major Tom, as if he didn't want to know what came next.

'What I mean is, I thought I had feelings for him, and because of that I felt I should at least hear his side.'

Will let out a snort at this, and then looked sheepish. 'Sorry,' he mumbled, so like a little boy that had been caught out that Megan couldn't help but laugh. Will joined her with a rueful grin.

'So I listened, and what he told me made up my mind.'

Will's eyes moved to her face, and she knew she had his attention.

'I think we had both fallen in love with our own ideas of what the other person was like. I didn't really know Greg, but now that I do — well, I know we aren't right for each other.'

Megan knew she could be wishing it had happened, but she could have sworn she saw some of the tension ease from Will's shoulders.

'I needed to know that I wasn't just lashing out in anger, and so I needed to speak to him one last time. His approach to life and mine, they are so different. Too different. For me, I approach life and business — ' She gestured at the cattery around her. ' — the same. Treat people how you want to be treated.' She shrugged. 'That's not how Greg sees things. And that's fine for him, but not for me.'

'Maybe now would be a good time to talk about the clinic,' Will offered.

'No need. I've heard Greg's side, and I know that your side will be different. I know deep down the person that you are, and I know you would never have done anything in business that was unfair.'

Will nodded.

'I knew the couple who owned those cottages for years. I also knew how desperate their situation was. Greg was offering them less than the market value, with the promise to keep the properties as they were. I knew different. As soon as they had moved, he was going to pull the cottages down anyway. So I offered them more money to cover their cost of care, so they could be comfortable. And I was honest with them. I told them right from the start what my plans were . . . ' Will's voice trailed off.

Megan reached out and placed a hand on his arm and gave it a squeeze.

'I suspected as much, but that is the

thing. You didn't need to tell me, because I trust you.' The words fell out of Megan's mouth before she could really think about them. She blushed a little at her own honesty, but knew that it was true. She did trust Will, possibly more than any other man in her life.

Will looked down at the ground, and Megan knew he was processing what she had said, so she stayed silent.

'I'm sorry about the whole notepad thing.' She knew she had already apologised, but felt like it needed to be said again.

'Not your fault,' he said, turning to look at her. 'I jumped to conclusions and didn't let you explain.'

They shared a smile now at their own foolishness. Megan opened her mouth to speak.

'I've got the chicken,' Chloe said as she walked into the pen, and Megan closed her mouth. That conversation would have to wait until after they had freed Major Tom.

26

Will placed the plate of chicken at the bottom of the fence, beneath the hole, and held out a piece near Major Tom's nose. He sniffed it suspiciously, as if it might be poisonous, and then nibbled it from Will's fingers. Will picked up another piece and wafted it slightly below Major Tom's nose. Megan felt sure she saw the cat roll his eyes, but he wiggled just a little in the right direction so that he could eat the tasty treat. It was slow progress, but with chicken to guide him, Major Tom managed to navigate his way to the hole that was waiting to free him from the fence.

When he was close enough, Will reached in and pulled the cat gently through the hole. Initially ruffled — and then purposely nonchalant, as if all that had happened had been entirely intentional — Major Tom walked over to the remaining chicken and scoffed the lot.

'I think it is safe to say he is none the worse for wear.' Will said with a smile. 'You just have to know what their favourite treat is, then you can pretty much get them to do anything you want.

'Top tip,' Megan said with relief. 'Chloe, could you keep an eye on him, and when he has finished put him in the free pen at the end? I'll let Graham know that we have some repairs to do.'

'Sure,' Chloe said, before turning her attention to Major Tom. 'I told you that cats weren't designed to go to space — that's monkeys!'

Will gave Megan a quizzical expression at this strange exchange, and Megan just made a 'Don't ask' gesture. They walked together down the corridor that separated the pens.

'Have you got time for a coffee?' Megan asked hopefully.

Will made a show of looking at his watch, and she tried not to let her smile show.

'I think I can squeeze in a quick one before my next client. That is, assuming you have biscuits?' he said with a cheeky grin.

'I think I can manage that,' Megan replied, and they walked towards the back door of the bungalow, which she had left open in her haste to get out to Major Tom. She stepped into the kitchen and stopped short. Will nearly collided with her. She moved to the side to let him stand beside her, and they both stared.

'What are you doing here?' Will demanded, since Megan seemed unable to speak.

'I'm here to discuss a business proposition with Ms Falstaff. Not that it's any business of yours.' Greg's voice was icy-cool.

Will turned to Megan, knowing that she needed to decide what happened next.

'I can't sell you the property, Greg. Even if I wanted to, if doesn't officially become mine for another ten months.'

'Yes, well, my solicitor feels there may be a way around that little problem.'

Megan arched an eyebrow. Auntie Cath's wishes were not a *problem* to *work around*. They were the last thing that she had asked of her, and there was no way Greg was going to convince her otherwise.

Megan clenched her fists and tried to take a steadying breath. She felt Will's hand on the small of her back, a comforting gesture as she tried to control the anger she felt, wondering what she had ever seen in Greg.

'I think you should leave,' she said through gritted teeth.

Greg looked from Megan to Will and shrugged.

'You might want to consider my offer, Ms Falstaff. I can assure you that it will be vastly more generous now than it will be in a year's time when you are desperate to sell.'

He picked up his briefcase which had placed on the kitchen table, smoothed down the front of his suit, and moved towards the door. Megan and Will both moved aside to let him go.

'If you come to your sense, ring my PA and make an appointment.' He held out a business card that Megan wanted to refuse, but her good manners won out, and so she took it from his outstretched hand.

Greg gave one more scathing look in Will's direction and then let himself out.

Megan felt like a balloon which had been deflated, and reached for a chair before sitting down heavily.

'And to think that you were ever taken in by his charms,' Will said and without looking, Megan knew he was grinning. She herself was staring at the business card.

'You're not seriously considering his offer?' Will asked incredulously.

Megan took a moment to think about whether she was or not. The real problem was that she wasn't sure she could see herself still living here, still running the cattery, in a year's time.

She knew that Auntie Cath had wanted her to give it a go, and she was determined to do that — but would she really be able to turn her back on nursing, her chosen profession, forever?

'No, of course not, it's just . . . ' Megan wasn't sure how to explain it.

'You're not sure that you want to live here forever?' he asked, pinpointing exactly what she was thinking.

The idea of turning her back on all that Auntie Cath had built made her feel suddenly terribly guilty but she also knew that Auntie Cath would want her to be happy. The two thoughts were overwhelming, and so was the sense of being all alone in the world. Megan pulled her arms tightly around herself to try and ease the sensation. She knew Will was watching her, giving her time to process. Quietly, he moved his chair so that he was sitting next to her, and threw one arm around her shoulders. In desperate need of some comfort, Megan leaned into him so that she could hear his heart beat in his chest, strong and steady.

'I don't want to throw away everything Cath worked for, but I'm not sure I can see myself doing this for the rest of my life.'

She felt Will nod.

'And that makes you feel guilty?' he asked gently.

Megan nodded back, knowing that she wouldn't be able to force any words from her throat, which had become tight with emotion.

'I wish she was still here,' Megan managed to say with her voice cracking. 'She was so wise, and always knew the right thing to say.'

Will pulled her close and held her tightly for a moment.

'And what do you think she would say if she was here right now?'

Megan smiled at the thought, and then laughed, as she could instantly picture Auntie Cath: hands on hips, shaking her head, and telling her to stop being daft.

'She would tell me that my life is

mine, and that I need to figure out what makes me happy.'

Megan felt Will smile.

'Sounds like Cathleen to me. Always ready with some good advice that actually requires the person to figure it out for themselves.

Now Megan smiled too.

'So all you need to figure out is what makes you happy. Sounds simple enough.'

Megan moved so that she could crane her neck and see Will's face, which was smiling. She shook her head. 'Only one of the hardest things in the world to figure out.'

'It is that. But it seems to me that staying here isn't all about the cattery. Chloe could probably run the place for you, and you could do something else. Unless it's Little River that puts you off.'

Megan thought about this for a few moments.

'I actually like it here, more than London.' That surprised her a little, as she hadn't really given London much thought since she had left.

'Well that might make the choice a little easier. Just don't let Ford pressure you into making a decision that you don't need to make right now. His motivation is purely selfish.' Will pulled away with a glance at his watch. 'I'll leave you to think about it. I have to go, or I will be late.'

'But we haven't had coffee,' Megan protested, even though she knew she was being a little unfair. She was rewarded with a smile.

'I should have thirty minutes between my afternoon rounds and evening surgery, so I could pop in then?' He tried to sound casual, but Megan was fairly sure that he wanted to come back as much as she wanted him to.

'Sounds good. If you're lucky, I might even make time to get to the bakery to buy some fresh buns.'

'In that case, I'm sold. See you about four.' And then he was gone.

27

At five past four, Megan was pacing again, but this time for an entirely different reason. Now she was impatient for Will to return as she had something to tell him. She looked over the table, all laid up ready with the makings of afternoon tea. Megan had been to the bakery and brought fresh scones, plus homemade jam and clotted cream from the local farm shop. After all she had been through in the last few months, she had finally come to some conclusions; and now Will, the first person she wanted to tell, was late.

Tinker and Belle shot through the cat flap with a tuneful chorus. Megan bent down and fussed them, but it seemed that their entry had heralded someone else's as the back door opened and Will stepped in. His work clothes were rumpled and there was mud splashes up the front of his chinos, but he wore a grin which told her that he had seen the tea things.

'Wow,' he said. 'I was thinking a coffee and a biscuit, not a lavish spread.'

Megan blushed a little. 'Well I wanted to say thank you for your help with Major Tom, and . . . ' She paused suddenly, feeling nervous, but not sure why. ' . . . I have something to tell you.'

Will's face changed from a grin to a cautious smile.

'Sounds intriguing,' he said as she gestured for him to sit.

'Tea alright, or would you prefer coffee?'

'I believe tea is the done things to drink on such occasions, so tea would be lovely.'

Megan busied herself putting the kettle on and moving the teapot.

'I can't wait for the tea, you're just going to have to tell me,' Will said, leaning forward in his chair with his elbows on the table.

Megan took a deep breath and

turned around so she was facing him.

'Well, I've thought about it, and I think that what I miss most is nursing.'

Will nodded, a sign she took as encouragement to continue.

'So I started thinking that maybe you were right. Perhaps I could keep Cath's Cats and also keep nursing.'

Will smiled now, and she could see light dancing in his eyes, which she took as his approval.

'So I did some research, and I'm going to visit the local community nursing team on Thursday. It would just be the occasional shift to cover holidays and sickness initially, but they think they might have a part-time job for me later in the year.'

Before she knew it, Will had made his way from his chair to standing in front of her and pulling her into a hug.

'I take it you think that's a good plan, then,' she said, laughing in to his shoulder. He held her for a few more moments and then stepped back so that they could see each other.

'The best news I've heard in a long time. I was hoping you would decide to stay.'

'You were?' Megan asked, biting her lip in anticipation for the words that she hoped were coming next.

'Oh, yes. Little River needs a decent cattery — and besides, at the rate you're going, you are going to keep me comfortably in business.' His look was innocent, but Megan knew him well enough to see when he was teasing her. She made a show of a mock punch to the arm and he stepped away, clutching his bicep and pretending he had been mortally wounded.

'Very funny,' she said, laughing, and trying to decide whether she should speak first. Will's face moved from amusement to seriousness, and Megan held her breath. He reached out for one of her hands.

'I don't think I could have borne it if you had told me you were leaving,' he said softly, and Megan felt pulled into his gaze.

'I don't think I could bear to leave you,' she said softly back.

Will nodded.

'As much as that is how I feel, I don't want to be the only thing that keeps you here.' There was deep sadness in his voice, and Megan felt relief that she could ease it. She stepped towards him and placed her free hand into his.

'You told me that Auntie Cath would want me to be happy, and that I needed to figure out what that was — and I have.'

The hopeful look in his eyes made her heart feel like it was going to burst.

'You make me happy, Will. Being here with you makes me happy. That's what I want. Once I had figured that out, all I needed to do was work out the rest. It made everything clearer some-how.'

As if he couldn't restrain himself any longer, Megan found herself pulled back in to Will's arms.

'I thought about nursing and the cattery,' she continued, knowing she needed to tell him everything, 'and I realised how lucky I am.'

'Oh, yes?' Will murmured.

'Yes,' Megan said. 'I can keep Auntie Cath's legacy going, and I can still nurse. And I can have you?' This last was more of a question, and she could feel the rumble of laughter build in his chest.

'I'm yours, if you want me,' he said. This time Megan pulled away, but only so that she could reach up and kiss him. Kiss this man that she had fallen in love with, for the first time.

The kiss was soft and gentle, but deep. Megan was sure she could have stayed in that time and place forever and been happy. Auntie Cath had been right — maybe she had even suspected that Will and Megan were perfect for each other.

Will pulled away. 'What do you think Auntie Cath is thinking right now?' He lifted a hand to brush strands of hair from Megan's face. She wondered again if he could read her mind.

'I suspect she is busy congratulating herself on being right as always,' Megan said, smiling. 'I wouldn't be surprised if this was her plan all along.'

'It was a most excellent plan,' Will whispered, before leaning in to kiss her once more.

We do hope that you have enjoyed reading this large print book.

Did you know that all of our titles are available for purchase?

We publish a wide range of high quality large print books including:
Romances, Mysteries, Classics
General Fiction
Non Fiction and Westerns

Special interest titles available in large print are:
The Little Oxford Dictionary
Music Book, Song Book
Hymn Book, Service Book

Also available from us courtesy of Oxford University Press:
Young Readers' Dictionary
(large print edition)
Young Readers' Thesaurus
(large print edition)

For further information or a free brochure, please contact us at:
Ulverscroft Large Print Books Ltd.,
The Green, Bradgate Road, Anstey,
Leicester, LE7 7FU, England.
Tel: (00 44) 0116 236 4325
Fax: (00 44) 0116 234 0205